"Don't try to sweet-talk me," Dani warned

"Why not?" Jack demanded, kissing the dimples at the base of her spine.

She jumped as if shot. "Stop that!" She batted him behind her back without turning around.

Smoothing his palms over her hips, he let out a gusty sigh. "This could be habit-forming."

"Listen!" Leaping up, she kept her back to him while she pulled on her clothes. "What just happened was a huge mistake. The truth is, I have no intention of getting serious about any man until I'm at least thirty."

"Who said anything about getting serious?" Frowning, he sat up. "That doesn't mean I intend to stop living, though." A significant glance at the bed conveyed exactly what he meant by "living."

"Whatever," she snapped. "I intend to forget this ever happened. I suggest you do the same."

"I don't think I can do that," he said, tracing the line of her jaw with his finger. And then he added what was obviously intended as a challenge. "I don't think you'll forget it so easily, either."

Dear Reader,

There are lots of ways to start over. My favorite is to tack a sign on your door declaring that you've "Gone to Texas," and then just take off.

Really. During the frontier days, that's exactly what discouraged Southerners and Yankees alike used to do when they flat gave up. Maybe they were dodging creditors or the law, but often they just wanted a fresh start. Whatever their reasons, they'd hang that sign, often abbreviated to G.T.T. and *go*.

Which is exactly what the Keene triplets do when they receive an unexpected inheritance: a dude ranch in the Lone Star state. Saying goodbye to Montana, Dani, Toni and Niki pack up and travel south with their beloved grandma. No pioneers ever had higher hopes of building new and better lives.

Only wise old Grandma dreams that new life will include so much love and laughter.

Welcome to Hard Knox, Texas, where the men are handsome, the horses are fast and the women are smart enough to appreciate both—eventually. *The Wrangler's Woman* is the story of the "smart" sister, but we've still got the "nice" sister and the "pretty" sister to go! Look for *Almost a Cowboy* in April and *The Cowgirl's Man* in May.

So welcome to the Bar-K Dude Ranch, folks. Y'all come back, hear?

Ruth Jean Dale

THE WRANGLER'S WOMAN
Ruth Jean Dale

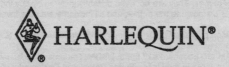

HARLEQUIN®

TORONTO • NEW YORK • LONDON
AMSTERDAM • PARIS • SYDNEY • HAMBURG
STOCKHOLM • ATHENS • TOKYO • MILAN • MADRID
PRAGUE • WARSAW • BUDAPEST • AUCKLAND

This book is dedicated to everyone
who's ever wanted to pull up stakes and start over.
Nothing ventured, nothing gained!

ISBN 0-373-25874-7

THE WRANGLER'S WOMAN

Copyright © 2000 by Betty Duran.

This edition published by arrangement with Harlequin Books S.A.

® and TM are trademarks of the publisher. Trademarks indicated with
® are registered in the United States Patent and Trademark Office, the
Canadian Trade Marks Office and in other countries.

Visit us at www.romance.net

Printed in U.S.A.

Prologue

ALL THE INTERESTING STUFF happened at the Elk Tooth Community Center.

The picturesque log structure at the edge of the little Montana town served as the site for parties and wedding receptions, political meetings and club gatherings, summer youth programs and holiday galas.

Tilly Collins, aka Mrs. Santa Claus each December for as long as anyone could remember, had seen them all during the past fifty years. But she'd never seen anything quite like the outpouring of woe on this particular occasion. And understandably so: a town as small as Elk Tooth could hardly enjoy saying goodbye to three of the most eligible women in the entire state of Montana—not to mention their always-ready-with-a-cookie-and-a-smile grandmother.

"Care for a cup of punch, Tilly?"

Mason Kilgore, the middle-aged photographer who also served as part-time manager of the local chamber of commerce, handed over a small paper cup. Tilly took it with a smile of thanks.

Mason shook his gray head in apparent disbelief. Sitting on the folding chair next to hers, he said mournfully, "I sure do hate to see you and the girls leave. I go out of town for two weeks and look what happens."

"Surprised us, too," Tilly admitted with a chuckle. "We had no idea what happened to the triplets' no-account pa after he deserted them and their mother all those years ago. This inheritance came out of the clear blue sky."

Mason grimaced. "I can't hardly blame them for wanting to claim a deluxe-type dude ranch, but in *Texas?*"

"Even in Texas." She nodded for emphasis. "It's the only decent thing Wil Keene ever did for his girls."

"When are you folks leaving?"

"Tomorrow morning. We've sent what we need ahead. Me 'n' the girls will drive down pulling a horse trailer." Now it was Tilly's turn to make a face. "Dani wouldn't go anywhere without that horse of hers."

"Don't blame her. That Appaloosa is worth a lot of money and she's smart enough to know that."

Tilly sought out Danielle across the crowded room. Oldest of the twenty-five-year-old Keene triplets, Dani was universally acknowledged to be "the smart one" of the bunch: the sister with the quick wit, the sharp tongue and the overdeveloped work ethic.

Dani stood near the punch bowl, deep in conversation with the middle-aged owner of the ranch where she'd worked for the past several years. Her brown eyes gleamed with intelligence as she nodded in understanding. Cute as a button, she wore the local costume—denim and boots—and she'd let wavy hair the color of chocolate fall free to the middle of her back.

Dani Keene was as pretty as she was smart, and her proud grandmother wasn't the only one who noticed.

"How's Toni taking it?" Mason inquired. "I know she's been going with that Barnes boy, but don't know if it's serious."

"Not on her part, anyway." Tilly knew, but didn't say, that Antonia had been looking for a way to let Tim Barnes down easy. She was known around this part of Montana as "the nice one" among the triplets, and this proved the point; she was too nice to hurt Tim's feelings with the truth. She'd had no romantic interest in him from day one, because he wasn't a cowboy.

Standing near the door, Toni give Tim Barnes an encouraging pat on the arm, her dark eyes distressed. There was a sweetness about Toni that everyone seemed to see at once, even before they noticed how attractive she was with her curly, light brown hair and pert figure.

Tilly glanced at the glum man beside her. "I guess the one you really hate to see go is Niki," she announced, not guessing at all.

"We'll never see her like in this town again," Mason said sadly. "Our loss is Texas's gain."

Tilly understood his cheerless state. Niki had worked for Mason for five years, both in his photography studio and at the chamber of commerce office. Known as "the pretty one," she'd won the Miss Elk Tooth contest three years running and she'd never even entered; Mason had entered *for* her. She'd probably still be Miss Elk Tooth today but she'd refused the title the fourth time it was offered.

Spotting Niki was easy, even in this crowd; she was always surrounded by men. Taller than her sisters, she wore her thick hair long and straight, cascading in a heavy fall all the way to her waist—and it was black instead of brown like theirs. She was the only one who'd got Wil Keene's blue eyes instead of their mother's brown ones, and where she'd got those cheekbones and long legs was anybody's guess.

Bottom line: Nicole Keene was the most drop-dead-gorgeous woman anyone in Elk Tooth had ever seen, and probably the most modest to boot.

Mason stood up, his knees creaking. "Guess there's nothing to be done," he said. "I better go see if the wife is ready to go home. Good luck in Texas, Tilly."

"Thanks, and good luck to you, too." She watched him thread his way through the crowd, thinking that Texas was sure to be a great adventure. She only hoped her granddaughters would find the happiness and security—the love—that had eluded them in Montana.

THE KEENE TRIPLETS and Grandma finished loading up the Jeep Cherokee on a blustery Montana March day. After hooking up the horse trailer and loading

Dani's prized Appaloosa gelding, they stood for a moment looking nostalgically at the little house on the edge of town. They'd called this place home for as long as they could remember—since before their mother's death in a riding accident when they were only seven. After that, it had been just Grandma and the girls all the way.

Toni sighed and shoved wind-tossed hair away from her cheeks. "Now that it's time to go—" her voice faltered "—I feel a little funny about leaving this old place. Do you think the new owners will be as happy here as we were?"

"Absolutely." Niki, managing to look gorgeous as usual without even trying, hugged her sister. "It's just an old house," she said encouragingly. "As long as we're together, it doesn't matter where we live. Besides, we'll have a better home in Texas."

"I suppose." But tears sparkled on Toni's lashes.

Dani grinned at her sisters. "I knew you two would get all choked up," she teased, "so I decided to do something about it. Wait right here!" She disappeared around the corner of the house at a run, heading for the little corral in back.

Her sisters looked at Grandma, who merely shrugged. Tilly had no idea what Dani was up to, but had faith that it would be something to cheer their departure.

Sure enough, Dani reappeared carrying a flat slab of wood. "Take a look at this," she said proudly, turning it so they could see what she'd written there in big black letters: GTT. Beneath that, in parentheses, she'd translated: Gone to Texas!

Toni frowned. "I don't get it."

"Because you slept through history class," Niki accused. "Early settlers posted signs like these on their doors when they pulled up stakes to head for the promised land. GTT—Gone to Texas!"

Toni giggled. "I never thought of Texas as the promised land," she protested.

"Well, it is," Dani declared. "We've fallen into the lap of luxury, ladies, and all we have to do is go claim it. One of you grab the hammer out of my coat pocket and the other help me hold this sign in place so we can nail it on the door."

This they accomplished with much giggling and horseplay. Then, flanking their grandmother, they stood arm in arm for one final look before piling into the Jeep.

"Gone to Texas!" Dani sang out as she turned the car and trailer south. "Hey, it worked for the pioneers and it'll work for us!"

In the back seat, Tilly sent up a silent prayer.

1

Texas barbecue was the *best* barbecue in the world, hands down. Jack Burke figured everybody knew that.

Since the Sorry Bastard Saloon in Hard Knox, Texas, served the best barbecue in the state, that's where local barbecue fans gathered. The saloon was packed with rowdy young cowboys and indulgent townfolk on this Saturday afternoon in March, Jack among them.

Until lately, the Sorry Bastard could also boast of having the best-looking barmaids in Texas, but recent marriages had thinned those ranks. Not that Jack Burke ever came in for the scenery, heck no.

"Hey!" One of the cowboys bellied up to the bar and yelled in Jack's face. "I said please pass the hot sauce!"

"Oh, sorry." Jack passed the dangerous red condiment, then carefully picked up the last sloppy bite of his barbecue-beef-brisket sandwich. "I was thinkin'."

"Yeah," the cowboy said wisely, "like we all been, I bet, about them Keenes comin' in to take over the Bar K. It's a real shame your daddy and grandpa won't be able to buy that place now. Just when they's gettin' close, old Wil Keene up and kicks the bucket."

This was greeted with somber nods all around. Everybody in the county had known old Wil Keene and none of them had liked him much, especially the Burkes of the XOX Ranch. Wil had been a cranky SOB, but his neighbors had coexisted uneasily with him for the sake of his wife.

Miss Elsie Knox had been revered locally as a kind lady from pioneer stock. Hell, the town of Hard Knox got its name from one of her great-great-something or others. Why an aging maiden lady had waited all those years for her prince to come and then up and married a carpetbagger like Wil Keene five years ago was anybody's guess. But she had, and out of respect they'd tried hard to get along with the abrasive foreigner plunked down in their midst.

They managed fairly well until Miss Elsie—no one ever called her Mrs. Keene—died. Then they moved in on Wil Keene like a flock of vultures, determined to rid themselves of a constant irritation.

The fastest way was to buy him out. Three ranchers whose land touched on Bar K borders made the widower offers they hoped he couldn't refuse, Jack's pa and grandpa among them. But Keene, who was getting up there in years and growing more surly by the minute, just sneered at all comers.

There was nothing for locals to do but stand by shaking their heads in collective disapproval while they watched the little Bar K go to hell in a handbasket.

Now Wil's three sons were coming in to take over the failing dude ranch, and nobody was very enthusiastic about *that*, either.

"Those Keene boys are due in any day now," one of the cowboys at a table near the bar offered. "Them ol' boys are gonna have a real job of work gettin' that place fit for dudes."

Joe Bob Muskowitz, the long drink of water at the end of the bar, nodded. "They'll play hell gettin' any help from around here," he predicted. "Their daddy ticked off just about everybody in this town at one time or another and they're probably just like him."

Heads nodded solemnly, all except Jack's. Disgusted with himself for doing it, he still felt duty bound to speak up. It was hell to be beholden to a man you disliked and then have him die before you could repay your debt of honor.

"Wil Keene wasn't—" he swallowed hard "—*all* bad."

"Wal, where's *that* comin' from?"

Joe Bob gave the speaker an incredulous glance. "Where you been? Remember when Jack's grandpa rolled his pickup last year? It was Wil who hauled the old man out just before the gas tank exploded—am I right, Jack? Saved Austin's life, sure as shootin'."

"That the way it was, Jack?" the other asked.

"Just about." Jack didn't like having his business

discussed in public, but what could you do in a small town like Hard Knox?

"I still wouldn't want to be one of them Keene brothers," Joe Bob said emphatically. "I heard all about 'em—triplets, somebody said. Names are Danny, Nicky and Tony. Ain't that sweet?"

"It's not their front names that bother me," the other cowboy said, "it's the last one—*Keene*."

"You got that right...never trust a Keene, just like their old man." There were knowing nods all around.

Jack figured he ought to stick up for Wil Keene, but how? If he hadn't owed Wil, he'd likely be making the same harsh judgments. And the thing was, Grandpa didn't drive a danged bit better today than he had when he flipped that pickup and put his grandson between this rock and a hard place.

"Now," he said halfheartedly, "don't be too hard on 'em before you even lay eyes on 'em. They could be real nice guys."

"From *Montana*?" Miguel Reyes, hitherto silent, raised his brows. "It's too cold up there. Makes people all pinched and pale." He looked at his own brown hand as if for emphasis.

"Yeah, and they talk funny, too," another chimed in. "Why, I heard tell—"

The outside door flew open and Dylan Sawyer, a young cowboy from the XOX, stuck his head inside. "Hey, everybody, the Keene kids are in town! I just saw a dusty Jeep with Montana plates pull into the parking lot at the Y'all Come Café! Let's go check 'em out!"

The bar of the Sorry Bastard emptied in a flash. Jack sat there for a moment longer, practically alone except for the lady bartender, who also happened to be the owner, Rosie Mitchell.

She looked at him, rolled her eyes and said, "Well, hell. There goes my Saturday business. At least *you* didn't run off on me."

"Don't get your hopes up, Rosie." Jack slid off his stool, digging in his jeans pocket for bills, which he tossed on the bar. "I may not like the Keenes any more than anybody else around here does, but I always pay my debts."

And the sooner, the better. All he wanted was to be done with the Keenes, the whole lot of 'em, once and for all.

THE Y'ALL COME CAFÉ WAS only a block and a half away, so Jack hoofed it. As he neared the little restaurant, he saw the last of the cowboy crowd disappear inside. It was almost enough to make him feel sorry for the Keene brothers.

All set to follow, he caught movement from the corner of his eye and turned to see a woman walk around the side of the building from the big back parking lot. She was leading just about the best looking Appaloosa gelding he'd ever laid eyes on.

She saw him, too. Their gazes met and all of a sudden he couldn't have told you whether that horse was a palomino or a bay. In her fringed leather jacket with a light wind ruffling her hair, she was even better looking than her horse, which was going some. He realized his mouth was hanging open and snapped it shut.

She raised slender brows in silent acknowledgment and turned away, the horse following obediently. Up and down she led the animal, obviously working out travel kinks. She must have just unloaded him from a horse trailer and was looking to his needs before seeing to her own.

Jack liked that. The woman must know horses. When she turned back in his direction the next time, he gave her a tentative smile. "Howdy," he said. "Just get into town?"

Beautiful chocolate-brown eyes widened incredulously. "Was that a lucky guess?"

"What can I say?" He shrugged modestly, playing her little game. "Are you just passing through?"

"That's right."

"Mind me asking where you're headed?"

"As a matter of fact, I do." She turned sharply and led the horse away from him again.

When she reached the outer limits of the small graveled area, she had no choice but to turn back again. When she did, he was waiting.

"Didn't mean to sound nosy."

"Well, you did." But she seemed somewhat mollified.

"I'd be happy to help you with your horse if—"

"Touch my horse and die!" Her eyes flashed; she had an extremely expressive face.

"Sorry!" He threw up his hands and backed up the steps to the front door of the café. "Just tryin' to be neighborly."

"Yes, well...whatever." The look she gave him said she wouldn't be at all surprised to find out he was actually a horse thief or worse, if there *was* anything worse.

This time when she turned away, he did, too. Nothing to be gained here. He might as well go on inside and gawk at the Keene brothers along with everybody else in town.

DANI WATCHED with skepticism as the tall, good-looking cowboy entered the café. At twenty-five, she'd lived long enough to know that strange men did not attempt to engage her in idle conversation without some ulterior motive. Usually it was to get closer to her sisters, but this guy hadn't even seen Toni and Niki yet so he must have been interested in Sundance, the Appaloosa she'd raised from a colt and trained herself.

Granny said Dani was too suspicious, but she didn't see how that was possible. All her life men had tried to use her to get to her gorgeous sisters, and all her life she'd seen right through them and sent them packing with her tart tongue and shoot-from-the-lip attitude.

Sighing, she led Sundance back around the building and loaded him into the trailer. He obeyed her commands with reluctance.

"It's almost over, old boy." She patted his speckled rump before banging the door closed. "Next stop, the Bar K!"

A little shiver of anticipation shot through her at the sound of it. All her life she'd wanted a ranch of her own, a place where she and her sisters and their grandmother could settle down and live happily ever after. Of course, Toni and Niki would get married eventually, but that was a long way away.

As for herself, she doubted she'd ever marry. After what their father had done to their mother, she couldn't imagine why *any* of the triplets would take a chance on a man. Toni, on the other hand, seemed unscathed by their father's desertion, to Dani's total amazement. As for Niki...Niki kept her own counsel in many areas.

All of which meant that Dani must be chary for all their sakes...but that cowboy *had* been tempting.

More than six feet tall, she judged, with wide shoulders and a lithe way of moving. Strong jawed for sure, but that was about all she could tell about his face, shadowed as it was by a brown Stetson hat. A working cowboy, obviously, in off the range for a little weekend fun and frolic.

She shocked herself by wondering if he needed a job, then gave a contemptuousness snort at the slightest inference that she cared.

Brushing off her hands, she entered the café

through the rear door. Emerging into the back of the dining room, she hesitated for a few moments, surveying the situation with her usual caution.

The Y'all Come looked as if it had started life as a Swiss Chalet. The steeply slanted roof was visible through windows framed by lacy wooden trim, and photos of snow scenes papered the walls. It was all so incongruous that Dani had to smile.

Then she stopped looking at the décor and honed in on her family.

Not too surprisingly, Niki and Toni were the object of considerable attention. They sat in a booth with Granny, chatting so animatedly that if you didn't know them, you wouldn't think they were even aware of the scrutiny of a whole roomful of mostly men.

Dani, *very* aware, was not pleased, especially when she spotted the nosy cowboy seated on a stool at the counter. He was watching her with an amused tilt to his lips. Lifting her chin, she stalked between the tables and slid into the only seat left in the family booth.

Everyone smiled, and Toni said, "How's old Sundance?"

"Old Sundance is fine." Dani picked up the mug of coffee they'd ordered for her. "Have you called the lawyer?"

Her sisters shifted a bit guiltily and Toni said, "We were just about to get around to that."

"Okay. Have you got directions to the ranch?"

"Well..." Toni and Niki looked at each other, and

Toni said, "Not exactly. The waitress is new around here and doesn't know, but I'm sure one of these nice cowboys can help us out."

Which was just what Dani didn't want to hear. Why did some women check their good sense at the door when men came on the scene?

"I CAN'T BELIEVE IT," Dylan Sawyer declared. "The Keene brothers turn out to be the Keene sisters! Does that take the cake or what?"

"It damn sure does," Jack agreed, watching the prickly woman he'd encountered outside march up to the booth in front of the window and sit down. "Dani, Niki and Toni—with an *i*. Got any idea which one is which?"

"Well..." Dylan licked his chops. "The pretty one—"

"Hell, they're all pretty." And they were, Jack realized, although none more so than the woman who'd been walking the horse. There was more to her than good looks, too. Intelligence just glowed from those dark eyes. Grandpa would call her smart as a whip.

"No, I mean the *real* pretty one, the one with that long black hair. She's Niki."

Jack looked at Niki more carefully, and somewhat belatedly realized what a knockout she was. Funny how he hadn't noticed anything special about her at first glance. "And the others?"

"The one in the red jacket is Toni, so the one who

just came in must be Dani—process of elimination," Dylan concluded with a guffaw. "They called the old lady who looks like Mrs. Santa Claus 'Grandma.'"

"Did you get identification on the horse?"

Dylan blinked. "What horse?"

"Let it go." A formal introduction, Jack was thinking. That's what he needed, seeing as Dani had seemed so leery of him. Hell, he was going to be neighbors with her—with all of them, he hastened to add. Might as well be friendly.

Joe Bob slid onto the stool on the other side of Jack's. "Man, did you get a load of that?" He jerked his head toward the women.

Dylan nodded, but then his look of eager anticipation faded. "They're still Keenes and that means they're off-limits," he said in a warning tone. "Damn shame, since they're so blasted cute."

"Yeah, a shame," Joe Bob agreed. "But lookin' won't hurt us any." And he banged Jack on the shoulder with a friendly fist, nearly knocking him off the stool.

A COWBOY WITH HANDS so big they dwarfed the coffeepot offered refills and bashful smiles all around.

Dani cocked her head and watched him slosh coffee over the rim of her chipped mug. "Don't quit your day job," she advised.

"Huh?" He seemed to be having trouble pulling his gaze away from Niki.

"Do you work here?"

"Naw." He chortled at the very thought. "I just wanted to get a closer look at y'all." Still laughing, he backed away.

"Wait a minute."

"Ma'am?"

Dani wanted to groan. She knew she must sound like a drill sergeant, but he didn't have to "ma'am" her. "Do you know where the office of an attorney named John Salazar is?"

"Yes, ma'am, I do."

"Well, would you mind telling *me* where it is?" she asked, exasperated.

"Oh. Sure." He pointed toward the front door. "Out there, turn right one block and left one block. It's in the Snake-oil Building—sorry, I mean the Snaesull Building, but we all call it the Snake-oil Building."

"Oh, lord." She rolled her eyes, then added a belated, "Thank you very much." To her family she said, "I'm going to walk on over so I can get the keys. Wait here and let the locals look you over. In fact, you probably should go ahead and eat."

Toni frowned. "Don't you want one of us to go with you?"

Dani shook her head. "If I need you, I'll come get you." She slid out of the booth. "I won't be long." She didn't wait for their response, knowing they'd acquiesce. She was, after all, the oldest of the triplets; she'd been born seven minutes ahead of Toni, who was born thirteen minutes before Niki, the baby of the family. Besides, business was Dani's forte, as being nice was Toni's and being beautiful was Niki's.

Dani just wished she was as good at her thing as they were at theirs.

DANI WALKED OUT the front door and Jack hopped off that stool and was after her like a shot. Wherever she was going, he'd just tag along in case she needed...anything, anything at all.

All in the interest of repaying a debt, of course. Nothing more.

By the time he got out the front door, she was standing at the curb, looking around with great interest. He trotted up to her with a smile.

"Looking for something?" he asked in his most winsome tone.

"Is that just another good guess?"

"Yep. Maybe I can help you."

"I don't need any help, thank you." She made a sharp right turn and walked quickly away from him.

He took that "thank you" as a good sign and followed. In a few long strides, he was beside her. She gave him an annoyed glance.

"Are you following me?" she demanded.

"No, ma'am, I'm being hospitable is all."

"Ohh!" She clenched slender hands into tight fists. "If one more person calls me ma'am—!"

"It's not your age," he explained. "It's your attitude. You are a tiny bit...intimidating."

She didn't miss a step. After about half a block, she

said, "You don't know me well enough to make that judgment. In fact, you don't even know my—"

"Dani Keene," he interrupted.

Then she *did* miss a step. "How did you know that?"

"Everybody does. We've been waitin' for the Keene brothers of Montana to roll into town and here you are. I'm Jack—"

"I don't *care* who you are." She crossed the street and he kept pace. "I don't take up with strangers on the street. If this is the way Texas men treat women—"

"Now hold it right there! Texas men don't take a back seat to *any* men in their treatment of women. I'm tryin' to be nice and helpful here, is all."

"What part of 'leave me alone' don't you understand?" She stopped so suddenly that he took a couple of steps past her. She was obviously checking out the two-story buildings in front of them.

"That one." Jack pointed.

She blinked. "That one, what?"

"You're lookin' for the Snake-oil Building—excuse me, the Snaesull Building, right?"

"Yes, but how did you know that?" She faced him with fists on her hips and suspicion in her eye.

"Because John Salazar is your attorney."

She looked on the verge of an explosion. "How do you know John Salazar is my attorney?"

"Because he was your father's attorney."

She almost flinched at the mention of her father,

and some of the fight went out of her. "What else do you know about m-my..." she swallowed hard, looking suddenly vulnerable "...my father?"

"Quite a lot, now that you bring it up." He wondered why she'd had so much trouble with the word *father*. "I grew up here and I've watched the Bar K...go through a lot of changes. If there's anything I can do to help you while you're here—"

"You make it sound like I'm on a vacation," she said. "I'm here to stay."

He nodded, pleased to hear it. "That's fine by me, but...things may not be exactly what you expect. All I'm saying is that if I can help, I'll be glad to do it. Any questions?"

She looked almost panicky for a moment, but a shaky breath seemed to steady her. "This isn't a good time. Look, Jack, I don't mean to seem unfriendly but I don't have the faintest idea who you are and I'm in no mood for company, anyway."

She remembered his name. That was a good omen. "Jack Burke, of the XOX Ranch, at your service." He put out his hand, hoping for a shake so he could touch her.

She ignored his outstretched hand. Her blank look said that the next time they met she probably wouldn't even remember him. "Thanks for your interest, but I have business to attend to. If you'll excuse me..."

What if he wouldn't? She didn't wait to find out, just wheeled and walked into the Snake-oil Building.

For a long moment, Jack stood on the sidewalk looking after her, thinking she might be as prickly as her old man.

But a whole helluva lot easier on the eyes.

BACK IN THE CAFÉ AGAIN, Dani sat down hard on the booth seat and looked at her startled siblings and grandmother. "He wasn't in," she said.

"The lawyer?"

Dani nodded. "His secretary gave me a set of keys and wished me luck. I got the feeling she thought I'd need it."

Toni picked up a french fry. "At least you didn't waste the walk."

"I needed the fresh air to clear my head." Not that it had succeeded. "I..." She saw the tall cowboy—Jack something or other, he'd said—at the counter again and she quickly turned her gaze away. The café had only emptied out a little. "I'm getting a funny feeling about this."

Toni and Niki exchanged glances. "Funny how?" Toni asked.

"Funny...like the ranch isn't all we're expecting it to be."

Granny leaned forward and patted her granddaughter's hand. "Don't be negative, dear. I'm sure it's wonderful."

"That's right." Niki nodded firmly. "We saw the brochures and brochures don't lie."

Dani had thought at the time that the brochures

looked at least thirty years old, but swept up in the excitement, hadn't mentioned that little qualm. "I'm sure you're right." She sighed. "It's just that this has been a long hard trip and I'm tired. You all must be, too."

Toni laughed. "Why should we be tired when you did ninety percent of the driving? Once we get to the ranch, you deserve a nice long rest, Dani."

"We all do." Somehow Dani didn't think any of them would get much rest, but she wouldn't rain on their parade. "Why don't I pay the check and we can get out of here? Until we see the place, we won't know what we're talking about."

"Uhh..."

"Uhh...what?"

Again those surreptitious glances, and Granny said, "It's a little complicated—the directions, I mean. There are two ways, the long way and the short way. The long way is complicated, but the short way is practically a secret, from what the lady who runs this place told us."

"Are you saying we need better directions?"

"Or a guide," Toni said, grinning. "Come on, Dani, cheer up! We're almost there—Gone To Texas! The promised land. Remember?"

"I remember." Dani told herself she was being ridiculous, but ever since that brief conversation with the cowboy, she'd had the oddest feeling that something wasn't quite right at the Bar K. "I'm just being silly," she added. "Stay here while I pay the bill and get decent directions."

Rising, she picked up the check and took the few steps to the cash register. She handed it to the pleasant-faced woman behind the counter, along with a twenty dollar bill.

The woman smiled and shook her head. "It's already taken care of," she said.

Dani frowned and glanced at the table. All three women shrugged; none of them had paid the check. "I don't understand," she said. "None of us—"

"Jack took care of it," the woman announced. "Y'all come back, hear?"

Jack. The cowboy. This couldn't go on. Dani marched up to where he sat at the counter, grinning.

She was steaming. "Look," she said shortly, "I can't let you do that. Tell me how much our bill was and I'll..." She fumbled her wallet out of the pocket of her jacket, hoping she'd have the exact change.

He shook his head. "My pleasure," he said.

"Dammit, Jack, you can't—"

"It's done. Short of making a scene, there's not much you can do about it." His calm, almost patronizing expression didn't waver.

Dani gritted her teeth and took a deep breath. He was right, but how dare he put her in this corner? "Okay," she muttered, "you win this one. Thank you very much, but don't you *ever* do this again."

"No, ma'am, I sure won't." Clear hazel eyes crinkled at the corners. "Anything else I can do for you?"

"There certainly—is."

His grin widened. "Just name it."

"Can you give me directions to the Bar K? My family seems to think it's at the end of a labyrinth or something."

"Umm, not too many labyrinths in Texas that I know of. It is a little tricky to find if you don't know your way around, though."

"You can draw me a map."

"I can do better than that." He rose from the stool.

"There *is* nothing better than that," she flared. "Wait. Grandma always has paper and pencil in her purse."

"Don't bother."

"But—"

"I'll lead you there."

"I don't want you to show me the way," she objected in alarm. She really hated how he was pushing in, mostly because she found him so damned attractive.

"Yes, you do."

"Don't tell me what I want!"

"Dani," he said in that lazy drawl, "you *do*, you just don't know it yet. Trust me on this—when you get your first look at the Bar K, you'll be damned glad to have me around."

Dani's stomach dropped to her knees and she could only stand in dumb alarm while he waltzed around her to introduce himself to her family. That lump of dread had just turned into a boulder.

2

KEEPING JACK'S PICKUP in sight, Dani drove down dirt roads, through miniforests, over hills, until suddenly the Bar K Dude Ranch lay spread out before them.

The *ramshackle* Bar K. A sudden silence fell, and then from the back seat of the Jeep, Toni uttered a faint, "Oh, *dear*."

A tight-lipped Dani braked in a large gravel parking lot in front of the ranch house. To the right lay several outbuildings and a barn; to the left a number of log cabins and a swimming pool, empty and sad in the March sunshine.

The first word that leaped into her head was *paint*. The Bar K was in dire need of paint, preferably many coats of it. The house itself, although a pleasant sprawl with a wide front porch running the entire length of the building, looked shabby and unloved. The outbuildings were equally neglected and the barn was practically gothic.

Granny cleared her throat. "You girls will be amazed at what a little elbow grease will do for this place," she announced in a determinedly cheerful tone.

"But the brochure...!" Niki wailed.

Dani opened her car door. "It'll look like the brochure again," she said grimly. "I'm afraid it'll take more than elbow grease, though."

"Whatever it takes," Toni said, "we'll see it gets it. We're not afraid of a little hard work."

"Or a lot, for that matter." Dani climbed out and stretched, trying not to give in to panic when she thought of the state of their bank account.

The road from Elk Tooth, Montana, to Hard Knox, Texas, had been a long one. Without waiting for the rest of them, she hurried around to open the door to the trailer and back Sundance out. By the time that was accomplished, everyone had alighted and Jack had joined them.

His expression, Dani thought, was evasive, to say the least.

"So what do you think?" he inquired, his tone guarded.

"Uhh..." Toni licked her lips. "It's a little more...run-down than I expected."

He nodded. "That's true, but the underlying structure is still strong. After Miss Elsie died, Wil did kind of let things go—" He stopped short. "I'm sorry, I don't mean to sound critical of your father."

"Feel free," Dani invited. Tossing the rope lead over the horse's neck, she grabbed a hunk of mane and swung up. After settling herself firmly on the bare speckled back, she turned the horse and tightened her knees to urge him forward.

They took off toward the trees at a slow lope, Dani

reveling in the rippling muscles between her thighs. All that pent-up power raised her spirits considerably.

So did the landscape. All her life she'd heard about the Texas Hill Country, and she wasn't disappointed. These rolling hills would be beautiful in the full flower of spring. So the buildings were not in the best of shape, the land was wonderful. What had she expected, the moon?

Not exactly *expected*. More like *wanted*.

Reining Sundance around, she supposed she'd been naive to believe that brochure. Still, the place was full of potential. It had been successful in the past and could be again. It all depended upon how badly they wanted it.

Dani wanted it more than anything in the world.

With a yell, she let out the tight rein she'd been holding on the Appaloosa's halter and he shot forward in a dead run. Wind whipped Dani's hair away from her face and she felt her spirits rise with every pounding hoofbeat.

This would work. She'd *make* it work. Nothing would stand in her way, not even the dangerously appealing cowboy waiting beside the barn.

DAMN, THE WOMAN COULD ride.

Jack watched the spotted horse sit back on his haunches in a sliding stop. Even bareback and guided only by a halter rope, the animal was under perfect control.

Dani jumped to the ground, her cheeks red and her eyes sparkling. He'd thought she was good-looking before, but he hadn't seen anything. This was the *real* Dani Keene, he knew instinctively, not that suspicious woman who'd cut him off back in town.

By the time she reached him, though, the joy had been replaced by caution. "This is beautiful country," she said, glancing around. "Sure, the ranch itself needs work, but it'll be worth it."

"I wondered if you'd see that." He patted the nose of the curious Appaloosa. "You got a real nice horse here."

Her smile revealed genuine pleasure. "He sure is. I raised him from a colt and trained him myself. We suit each other just fine."

"The corral's empty. You can put him in there."

She frowned. "Don't we have any stock at all?"

"Some. Dobe can tell us how much."

"Dobe?"

"Dobe Whittaker. He's kinda the caretaker, you could say. He's around here some—"

"I'm where I'm s'posed to be." A man stepped from the deep shadows of the open barn door. Looking as old as the hills, he wore cowboy clothes softened by age. The stamp of the West was in far-seeing blue eyes and a lined, leathery face partially concealed by a snowy beard and trailing mustache.

"Howdy, ma'am." He doffed his hat. "I'm Dobe Whittaker. At the moment you got a dozen horses and a small herd of longhorns and that's just about it."

"Dobe." She smiled, genuinely pleased to meet him. "I'm Dani Keene. My sisters and grandmother are back at the house."

"Seen 'em go in." Without waiting for a response, Dobe wheeled back into the shadows.

Dani looked at Jack, her forehead furrowed. "Not very friendly, is he?"

"Depends on who he's dealin' with."

"He doesn't know me well enough to dislike me," she pointed out.

"He knew your dad."

She walked past him, leading the horse toward the corral. "If he disliked my father so much, why is he looking out for things?"

"Because of loyalty to Miss Elsie." Jack was still cautious about criticizing Wil Keene.

"I see." She said it so grimly that Jack thought maybe she did see.

Opening the gate, she slipped off the halter, and Sundance trotted inside. Making straight for a patch of dirt stomped and mashed by a multitude of horses before him, he lowered himself and rolled.

When she looked at the horse, her expression softened. Jack wished it would do the same when she looked at him, but so far that hadn't happened.

Squaring her shoulders, she faced him. "Will you bring Dobe up to the house to meet the rest of the family?"

"I'll try." In actual fact, he wasn't at all sure Dobe was interested in meeting any more Keenes.

"Thank you." She turned and walked away, covering the ground between barn and house with long, easy strides.

He watched with admiration. She might be a foreigner, but she was no stranger to ranch life. If it was possible to make a go of this run-down dude ranch, Dani Keene was the woman who could do it. Although Jack's father and grandfather were still determined to own this place, Jack would help her in every way he could.

Or more accurately, in any way she'd let him.

He turned toward the barn and hollered. "Dobe! Come on out here, you old reprobate."

Dobe shuffled out immediately, his grin sheepish. "Howdy, Jack. What you up to, comin' in here with them *wimmin*?"

"Just bein' neighborly." They shook hands and then Jack patted the smaller man on the shoulder. "You might give it a try yourself."

Dobe snorted. "Not hardly. I done my duty by Miss Elsie because nobody else would. Now I'm pullin' up stakes. I don't want nothin' to do with no more Keenes, no sir-ee-bob, I don't."

"You got 'em all wrong, Dobe." If he couldn't talk the old man into staying, Dani's row was going to be even harder to hoe. Dobe had earned the respect of the cowboy community, and if he refused to hang around, who would? "They're real nice, those Keene sisters and their grandma. Don't you think you could cut them a little slack?"

"Nope." The old cowboy shook his head decisively. "I'm leavin' pronto, already packed and ever'thin'."

"And going where?"

Dobe blinked. "I can find a job," he declared defensively. "Don't you worry about me none."

Realizing he'd taken a wrong approach, Jack nodded. "It's not you I'm worried about, it's the Keenes. They need you, Dobe, whether they know it or not."

"Yep, but I don't need them."

"Why not? They'll pay you a fair wage—" Jack assumed they would "—and they're smart enough to realize you know the lay of the land and they don't." He hoped.

"They ain't got a prayer of gettin' this place back on its feet," Dobe scoffed.

"Not without you," Jack said, buttering up the old codger. "How about giving them a chance?" When that didn't bring instant acquiescence, he added, "As a personal favor to me."

Dobe thought that over. Then he let out a disgusted snort. "When you put it that way, I don't have a whole lotta choice. You always been square with me so... Okay, Jack, I'll do it as a favor to you. But if they turn out to be anything like their old man, I'm outa here, no ifs, ands or buts."

"Fair enough." Jack felt great relief. "How about

comin' up to the house with me so you can meet the rest of them?"

"Okay, but I ain't gonna like 'em."

You might, Jack thought. *That grandma could be just your type.*

"THE HOUSE HAS TONS of possibilities," Toni announced.

"And some of this furniture is wonderful." Niki ran a hand over the dusty arm of a leather chair with armrests made of animal horns. "I wonder how old this stuff is."

Dani, who was much more interested in the outdoors than the indoors, looked up from the old ledgers she'd pulled from a desk drawer. "Could be from the twenties. That's when dude ranching really took off in a big way, according to the research I've done."

Toni looked around with surprise. "Gosh, I didn't know you'd done *research.*"

"It's an interesting subject." Dani closed the book and leaned her elbows on it. "For instance, dude ranching got started in the late nineteenth century. A lot of people from back East visited friends in the West, and sometimes they stayed and stayed and stayed. When it got too expensive for the ranchers to support all those frequent guests, some of them started charging and voilà! The dude ranch was born."

"I don't know about that." Toni looked worried. "It doesn't sound too nice to charge your friends."

"Oh, dear," Granny exclaimed. "Don't let Toni handle the billing or we'll be broke in a month."

Everyone laughed. Opening a drawer, Dani pulled out a wad of papers. Old bills, mostly, but when she unfolded a piece of lined notepaper it revealed a scrawled message: "Are you having fun yet? You girls don't know half as much as you think you do."

"What in the world?" she wondered aloud. "Granny—?"

The front door opened and Jack walked in, leading the old cowboy she'd met briefly at the barn. Hastily stuffing the piece of paper in her jeans pocket, she stood up to greet them.

While Jack made the introductions, she tried to calm her jangled nerves. Finding the unsigned note had upset her because she was sure her father had written it. Reading it had been like hearing his voice from the grave. While he was alive he'd had no interest whatsoever in his daughters, leaving Elk Tooth before they were born and never so much as contacting them afterward. It had been a shock to learn he'd left them this dude ranch, but she'd supposed he'd had no one else to pass it on to.

Now she wondered if he'd simply lured them here to torment them from the netherworld.

"And you met Dani at the barn."

She smiled automatically and nodded, pulled back into the here and now. Dobe wasn't looking at her anyway, but at Granny. And he wasn't smiling, he was glowering.

So was she, Dani saw with surprise. Grandma, who liked everybody and was liked by all in return, did not look impressed by Dobe Whittaker. It didn't take much to figure out why, either.

If Grandma looked like Mrs. Santa Claus, Dobe was the spittin' image of *Mr.* Santa Claus. Tilly Collins didn't like that, not one little bit. He was stealing her thunder, and worse, he'd got here first.

Dani intervened quickly. "So when will it be convenient for you to show me around?" she asked the old cowboy.

Dobe slanted a skeptical glance at Jack. "About anytime, I reckon. Maybe you can all come so I'll only have to do it once. I'll round up the horses and—"

"Not me," Niki said quickly.

"Beg pardon?"

"I'm not a horse person."

"Missy, this is a dude ranch. Horses are a real big part of it."

Niki's expression grew uncharacteristically stubborn. "There are a whole lot of things in this world that I can do happily, but messing with horses isn't among them. Count me out, please."

Dobe rolled his eyes expressively, but all he said was, "It's up to you, missy. Tell you what, I'll be ready first thing tomorrow morning and anyone who wants to come along is welcome."

"Thank you," Dani said. "And thank you for taking care of things after...after our father died. We do appreciate it."

"Yeah, well..."

"You'll be staying on with us, won't you?"

Silence greeted her question, and Dani found herself holding her breath. They were starting so deep in a hole that without the continuity Dobe could provide, she couldn't imagine what they'd do.

He let out his breath on a gusty note. "I'll stay for a while anyway, till we see how it goes. In the meantime, I got chores."

Turning, Dobe stomped out of the house. After a moment's silence, Dani laughed a bit shakily. "Another crisis averted."

Jack stirred. "Naw, no problem, he's always like that. Just treat him fair and he'll work his heart out for you. He goes back a real long way with this place so I think he can tell you a lot of things you need to know."

"I'm sure you're right."

For another long moment, she met his gaze directly, until a slight feeling of unease skittered up her spine. Looking down abruptly at the messy desktop, she said faintly, "Well, if you have to leave now... I mean, you've been very helpful, but I'm sure we've already intruded on your time quite enough."

Jack said, "I can take a hint." Turning toward the door, he put his hat back on his head. "If there's anything else I can do for you—"

"You've done quite enough already." The words sounded considerably more impatient than she'd intended.

"See you around, then. Ladies..." His nod included them all and then he was gone.

Everyone looked at Dani with various degrees of puzzlement. Then Toni said, "Gosh, he's cute," which pretty much broke the tension.

THE WOMEN HELD a war council that night over a supper of canned soup and crackers. They were all in complete agreement: their futures depended upon making the Bar K pay, so they'd knuckle down and work their fingers to the bone if need be.

Dani, proud of the lot of them, nodded approval. "It will be tougher because money is so short," she said, "but when wasn't it?"

"Money can't buy happiness, anyway," Toni said blithely.

"That's only your opinion," Dani snapped back. Softening her tone, she added, "It is a little strange that no money came with this place. With what we cleared for the house in Montana, though, we should be able to make it, God willing and the creeks don't rise."

"I can get a job," Niki said suddenly.

Dani frowned. "Are you sure you want to do that? I mean, with all that has to be done here, you'd be working night and day."

"It won't be that bad. Besides, we need the cash."

"I'll bet they'd hire you at the chamber of commerce," Toni predicted. "Remember what Mason said? You're the best advertisement a town can have and you even have experience."

Niki made a wry face. "I don't want to do that again. I just want a job where I can maybe make a little money. Unfortunately, I'm not loaded with qualifications."

"Tips," Toni declared. "You need a job where you can get tips. All those cowboys at that café were just falling all over you. Maybe you could be a waitress?"

Niki perked up. "Or a barmaid." She glanced at Dani. "Maybe we can ask Jack for—"

"Leave Jack out of it, why don't you." It sounded terribly ungracious, but that was how Dani felt. "I'm sure you can get any job you want without his help or anybody else's. But a barmaid...I don't know. I'm not so sure that's a good idea."

Her two sisters exchanged puzzled glances, but let it pass.

"While we're splitting up jobs," Tilly said, "I'll handle the cooking and the kitchen, of course."

"I'll be Grandma's assistant," Toni said eagerly. "I can manage the housework, so once we get this place in shape, I'll be the maid." She grinned broadly. "And Dani will handle the business end of things, of course, and take care of all the outdoors stuff."

"And," Niki interjected, "when I'm home I'll do whatever's needed as long as it has nothing to do with horses."

Nods of understanding greeted this pronouncement. Niki's fear of horses was well known in the family; they understood its roots and accepted it with regret.

"All right," Dani said decisively. "Tomorrow's Sunday, so Niki and I won't be able to get anything done in town until the next day. Then, while she fills out job applications, I'll put an ad in the newspaper. We need wranglers and we need them bad if we hope to be ready for the first guests."

Granny blinked. "What first guests?"

"These!" Dani held aloft a handful of reservation forms. "I found these in the desk in the big room in front—the great room, I guess you'd call it. Apparently there are quite a lot of people who come here every summer and have for years. If we can just pull everything together in time... But it'll take help, so it's important that we get the ad into the newspaper right away."

"Hey," Toni said with a smile, "things are looking up!"

"Don't count your chickens," Dani warned. "We can't let down our guard for a minute. Don't forget, this is Texas. It's a man's world down here. You saw how those guys swarmed around you today? Well, don't let 'em fool you. If you give any of them an inch, he's sure to take a mile."

"Really?" A very faint smile curved Niki's lips. "Are you thinking of anyone in particular, maybe someone like that good-lookin', slow talkin' Jack Burke?"

Dani felt hot color rush into her cheeks. She lifted

her chin with hauteur. "I'm speaking of men in general. Which reminds me..." She dug around in the pocket of her jeans and pulled out a scrap of paper, which she offered to Granny. "Do you think Wil Keene wrote that?"

Granny's eyes widened and she smoothed out the wrinkles, then read aloud, "Are you having fun yet? You girls don't know half as much as you think you do."

Niki and Toni gasped in unison. "Where did you get that?" Niki demanded.

"Found it in the desk. Granny, do you think that's his handwriting?"

"Mercy, your guess is as good as mine. He wasn't big on writing letters, you know."

They did indeed.

"But..." Granny pursed her lips. "If you ask me, it sounds just like him—are you having fun yet! It's like...like some kind of *clue* to something. What in the world has that man done now?" She shook her head with obvious disgust.

And who could blame her? It was her daughter, twenty-five years younger than Wil Keene, who'd fallen for the fast-talking con man, been seduced and abandoned in short order. Granny had said over and over through the years that she would be eternally grateful her granddaughters had better sense.

"We won't worry about it," Dani decided for all of them. "We have too many important things to do to waste any thought or effort on a note that might not have been written by him at all. So who wants to do the grand tour with Dobe and me tomorrow morning?"

The answer was exactly nobody.

SUNDAY BREAKFAST at the huge XOX Ranch was a four-generation affair: Austin the grandfather, Travis the father, Jack the son, and Petey the orphaned, four-year-old grandson, whose parents had died tragically when he was still an infant. Gathered around the big wooden table in the dining room, they ate and argued and generally gave all-male households a bad name.

The Sunday menu never varied: chicken fried steak with home-fried potatoes, two or three fried eggs on each plate, with cream gravy over the whole thing. Jack figured if it didn't clog your arteries and kill you, you were just lucky.

Petey dropped his spoon on the floor and looked expectantly at his uncle, a stubborn brown cowlick hanging across his big hazel eyes.

"Get it yourself," Jack said. "I'm tryin' to teach you to be independent, kid."

"Ha!" Grandpa Austin snagged another huge slab of fried meat off the platter. "You help that boy, Jack."

Travis poured coffee into his cup and his father's. "You're spoilin' the boy, Pa. Jack's right."

Petey just sat there grinning from one to the other; he always enjoyed stirring up the pot. When his glance snagged on his uncle Jack's, the grin slipped.

He hopped off his chair to pick up the spoon, which he put back on his plate without even wiping it off.

Jack figured the boy had already met and conquered every germ on the XOX, so he let it pass.

Austin fixed Jack with a gimlet eye. "I hear them Keenes are in town," he said.

"That's right." Jack hacked at his fried eggs with the edge of his fork. "Got in yesterday. Turns out they're daughters, not sons."

"Heard that." Travis speared a chunk of steak. "That'll make it easier to do what we're afixin' to do."

Alarm flared in Jack. "And what might that be?"

"Buy the place, same as always."

"Oh, that."

"We'll be doin' them a favor." Austin piped up. "It'd be hard enough for three able-bodied men with deep pockets to save that place. For three women it'll be dang nigh impossible."

Travis nodded. "I heard on the grapevine that no money come with the place so they gotta be strapped for cash. Seems kinda strange to me, though, all things considered."

"Well..." Jack's appetite was fading. "They—"

A crash shocked all thought out of him and he swung around to find Petey grinning while milk from his smashed glass traveled quickly across the hardwood floor.

"Doggone it, Petey!"

Muriel appeared, mop in hand. "I'll handle this," she announced, fixing the little culprit with a condemning eye. "Did you do that on purpose, Peter Burke?"

Petey caught his lower lip between baby teeth and shook his head solemnly. "No, ma'am," he said. "I just goofed."

Muriel's scowl transformed into an unwilling grin. "I swear, you take after the rest of the men in your family," she declared, flopping mop strings around in the white mess. "Just get by on charm, which is what all you Burkes do."

Grandpa winked at son and grandson. "Charm only gets us so far, right, fellas?"

Travis shrugged and Jack groaned. His grandfather had been married and divorced three times, and his father twice. One of the main reasons Jack had never taken the marital plunge was because of the rotten family track record where women were concerned.

When Muriel had withdrawn, Travis returned to the subject at hand without missing a beat. "The thing I don't get is, what happened to all Miss Elsie's money and family jewels? Even a fast worker like Wil Keene would have had trouble blowing it all in less than two years. If he was spending big money, it sure wasn't on anything a man could see, especially not that ranch."

"He coulda been a closet gambler," Austin speculated. "Or maybe he invested in a lot of bad stocks. I seem to recall a certain someone who tried to invest

in the awl bidness a buncha years back and got took
to the cleaners."

Travis lowered his brows in warning; his losses
had been so large that the entire family was in an up-
roar about it for months. Jack had been a kid at the
time, but he remembered it well.

"Whatever," Travis said. "Keene was stupid not to
sell that ranch when he had the chance. It sure
woulda spared them women a whole lot of grief."

"I don't know," Jack said mildly. "They seem awful determined to make a go of it, and I, for one, wish
them well." He was thinking of Dani and the intensity of her determination to make the Bar K a success.
Surely anyone who cared that much could make almost anything work. "It may take a miracle but...I
think the Keene sisters might be able to make something out of the Bar K again."

Austin obviously did not see it that way. "You're
pulling my laig." He scowled at his grandson. "They
couldn't make a go of it even if they had plenty of
money behind them, which they ain't. Besides which,
nobody's gonna work for them, just for starters. And
where, I ask you, are they gonna find dudes? Us, on
the other hand..." He puffed out his chest. "We're
turnin' reservations away."

"Maybe we should turn a few of them toward the
Bar K."

"Not only no, but *hell* no. Look, you just tend to
your own knittin' and stay away from them girls.
Women are nothing but trouble, as ever' last one of us

knows to our sorrow. And them Keene women are bound to be twice as bad."

"I don't happen to agree."

Splat! A big glob of gravy struck the rim of Jack's plate and splattered across the shiny wood beyond the plastic place mat. He looked up sharply to find Petey holding a spoon catapult fashion in his chubby, childish hands.

His smile was beatific and he said but a single word: *"Oops!"*

3

"BAR K DUDE RANCH, Toni Keene speaking."

"Hi, Toni. It's me, Jack. Is Dani around?" He'd expected her to answer and hoped his disappointment wasn't obvious.

"Uh-uh, and neither is Niki. They've gone to town."

"What for?"

She laughed; Lord, she really *was* nice. "Niki's looking for a job and Dani's going to put an ad in the newspaper."

"What kind of ad?"

"A wrangler wanted ad. Heaven knows we need help around here, and when the guests start arriving..."

He practically heard her shrug. "It's kinda late in the season to be hiring men," he said. "That may be a problem."

"I sure hope not." But her worry came through loud and clear. "We've got so many other problems that we don't need another one." She sighed. "Whatever—Dani will think of something. She always does."

Jack thought maybe he could "guide" Dani in the

right direction, but what he said was, "What kind of job is Niki looking for?"

"Whatever she can find. Maybe waitressing? She's very conscientious and could probably make good tips."

She could probably make good tips if she just stood in the middle of a room and smiled, he thought. "I don't doubt it for a minute," he said.

"That's why nobody's here but me and Grandma. Is there anything I can do for you, Jack?"

"Not really. I just wanted to...know if I could give Dani a hand with...anything."

"That's real nice of you," Toni said. "Guess you'll have to ask her. All I can tell you is that we're loving this place more every minute we're here. Sure, we have a lot of work ahead of us, but we're doing just fine."

"Glad to hear it. Nice talkin' to you, Toni."

Jack hung up and stood there for a few minutes, considering. He had a lot of work to do today, including the movement of several longhorns into the holding pen for shipment to Colorado day after tomorrow. Work on the XOX was never done. Besides the ranching operation, they bred a number of exotic species for sale to other ranchers, to zoos and farms. Herding dudes was the least of their endeavors. He'd often thought they should just give it up entirely, but the facilities were there, the cabins and recreation room and the swimming pool—

The telephone rang and Jack picked up automatically.

"This is Dr. Coleman. I'd like to reserve a week in June for myself and my wife at your guest ranch again this year."

"Howdy, Doc. This is Jack."

"Jack! Good to speak to you."

"Maybe not." *Grandpa will kill me for this*, Jack thought. "I'm afraid we're full up in June."

"Damn! I told my wife to call sooner, but she—"

"Yeah, well, I might be able to help you out, anyway." Jack switched the phone to the other ear and glanced around to make sure no one was listening. "There's another dude ranch just a few miles away that might have room for you. It's the Bar K, and I'm pretty sure you and the missus would really enjoy it...."

DANI AND NIKI CONFERRED in front of the *Hard Knox Hard Times* newspaper office on Main Street. A light wind whipped through, tossing their hair about their faces as they talked.

"While I place the ad, you can read the classifieds," Dani suggested. "Then if there's anything promising you can go check it out while I pick up supplies."

"Sounds good to me." Niki sighed. "God, I hate job hunting."

"If you don't want to do this—"

"Oh, no, I love working. It's *finding* work that bothers me." Niki grinned. "Maybe because I haven't had to do it very often."

"Like once," Dani said with a laugh. "After the Elk Tooth Chamber of Commerce got hold of you, it took a move to another state to pry you loose. At least you'll get a good reference."

"Somebody needs a reference?"

Jack; Dani realized with disgust that she knew his voice from the very first syllable, even when it came from behind her.

Niki smiled. "Hi, Jack. Fancy meeting you here."

"Uh-huh." He joined their circle. "Do I understand you're looking for a job, Niki?"

She nodded. "You wouldn't happen to know of one, would you?"

"As a matter of fact, I do. Ever been a barmaid?"

"No, but I wouldn't mind trying if it's a respectable bar."

"Niki!" Dani gave her sister a disapproving look. "I think you'd be much better off in a restaurant."

"Really?" Niki appealed to Jack. "*Is* it a respectable bar?"

"The most respectable," he assured her. "It's the Sorry Bastard over there." He pointed.

"Love the name," Dani said dryly.

"I think it's funny," Niki protested. "And you say they need help?"

"Two of the barmaids have quit in the last month to get married. You'd be greeted with open arms." He cast a surreptitious glance at Dani. "Of course, you could probably get on at the Y'all Come but you wouldn't make half as much in tips."

"I'm working for money, not love," Niki said emphatically. She glanced at her wristwatch. "It's only nine o'clock. When the Sorry Bastard opens, I'll just—"

"You don't have to wait for it to open. Go around back to the service entry and tell 'em Jack sent you. The owners are Rosie Mitchell and her husband, Clevon. Good people."

Niki's smile could stop traffic. "Thanks, Jack. You're a doll!"

Dani watched her sister turn away, pause at the street and then dash across with light steps. Annoyed with Jack, she said, "I sure hope this is no bum steer."

"Hey, would I burn you?" He looked at her with perfect innocence. "She'll make more money at the Sorry Bastard than working any other job in town."

"You mean because she's so drop-dead gorgeous."

"Hey, it's a beginning."

His crooked smile was so whimsical that Dani had to return it, however reluctantly. "Okay, I get it. Now if you'll excuse me—"

"To do what?"

"I have to place an ad in the newspaper."

"For what?"

"Dude wranglers."

He sobered. "It's kinda late in the season for that. You may have trouble—"

"Hold it right there." She squared her shoulders

and looked at him through narrowed eyes. "I've *got* to find a couple of wranglers to—"

"Three would be better."

"But I'll have to settle for what I can get." And afford. "You wouldn't happen to know of anyone looking for a job?"

"Only your sister. There may not be a cowboy in the county who'd be willing..." For some reason he was suddenly struggling to find words. "I mean, everybody's already working and even if they weren't..."

"If there's one thing I don't need, it's that kind of negative talk," Dani said firmly. "I happen to think you're wrong. I happen to think that when push comes to shove, something...something serendipitous happens and we get what we need."

"I sure hope you're right."

"But it's obvious you don't think I am." She planted her hands on her hips and glared at him.

"I *hope* you are but...no, I don't think it'll be that easy."

"Jack," she said, "let me tell you something about the Keene sisters. *Nothing's* ever been easy for us, up to and including this trip to Texas."

"When the going gets tough," he said softly, "the tough get going. Is that your point?"

"Close enough. If you don't have something positive to say, I'd appreciate it if you'd say nothing."

"Even if—"

"Even if nothing. When I want something, I go after it—and I want wranglers!" She turned away, still steaming. "See you around, Jack."

And she marched into the *Hard Knox Hard Times*, closing the door in his face.

NIKI WAS WAITING on the sidewalk when Dani exited the newspaper office fifteen minutes later. "I got it!" she announced, beaming from ear to ear. "Rosie— she's the really nice lady who owns the place—Rosie was all set to hand me an apron and put me to work on the spot, but I told her tomorrow was soon enough."

"That's great, Niki." Dani hugged her sister. "You're certain it's a decent place?"

"Oh, sure." Niki shrugged off all such concerns. "It's actually as much a restaurant as a bar, only wait-resses make more money on drinks than food. Best barbecue in Texas!"

Dani laughed. "I'll just bet it is." Arm in arm, the sisters walked toward the Jeep parked at the curb.

"You placed our ad?" Niki inquired.

"It'll be in tomorrow."

"And we'll get lots of applicants, I just know it." Niki squeezed the arm linked with hers. "Dani, everything's going to be all right now. We've had some hard times, but we've always managed to stick together. Sure, there's a lot of work still to be done, but as long as there's the three of us—four counting Grandma—nothing can stop us."

Dani was more than willing to believe that was true. If only she could get Jack's warning tone out of her mind...

DANI'S AD STIRRED UP exactly two calls.

The first sounded genuine enough, and everything was going just fine when all of a sudden the man backed off as if he'd been snake bit. Dani couldn't figure it out. When no other calls were immediately forthcoming, confusion turned to fear.

The second call came days later and it took all of five seconds to know the man didn't have the qualifications to *be* a dude, let alone wrangle one. Dani hung up with a sinking feeling in the pit of her stomach that refused to go away.

At the next family conference, she announced what she called "Plan B."

"Flyers," she explained. "I'll post flyers all over town. And Niki, when you're at work can you start mentioning to every cowboy you see that we're looking for— Why are you shaking your head at me?"

"Because I've been doing that all along and nobody's interested. It's like..." Niki frowned. "It's like we've been *blacklisted* or something."

"Blacklisted." The word went through Dani like a cold chill. "You don't suppose..."

"Oh, no." Toni sounded shocked. "These are nice people. I'm sure no one would actually work against us."

As one, the three turned toward their grandmother.

She frowned. "I wouldn't want to think there was a conspiracy," she said slowly, "but it really is strange that everyone's so standoffish. No one has dropped by to welcome us to the neighborhood, no one has asked if they could help.... Texans are famous for their hospitality, so you do have to wonder."

The sick feeling that seemed to follow Dani grew more pronounced. "I've kind of wondered." She looked around the solemn circle. "The Bar K is a small fish in a big pond. I don't see how we could be a threat to any of the other dude ranches, but what if... What if there was some reason we don't know about?"

Toni looked skeptical. "Such as?"

"Such as...well, like some big rancher wanted to buy us out. Or...or like we have a fortune in oil on our land and don't know it."

"Or maybe we control the water rights to this part of the state," Niki suggested, getting into the spirit of the thing.

Toni grinned. "Maybe they think we'll bring in sheep! The cowman and the sheepman can't be friends, you know."

Granny laughed. "That's the cowboys and the farmers, hon, but the point's well made. There must be some reason we're being treated like pariahs. Guess we'll just have to find out what that reason is."

"And in the meantime," Dani said, rising from the conference table, "we've got to find some men. We're about to work ourselves and poor Dobe to death."

"That old faker," Granny scoffed. "I wouldn't worry about him."

"Hey, Gran, he's all we've got at this point. I'm going into town right now to tack these flyers on every empty spot I can find. Wish me luck, okay?"

But even as she said it, she knew it would take a great deal more than luck.

JACK READ THE FLYER over Dani's shoulder as she tacked it to the light post: "Wranglers Wanted For Dudes. Competitive Pay, Excellent Working Conditions On Established Dude Ranch. Experience Desirable But Not Necessary. Contact Dani Keene At—"

She started and hit her thumb instead of the nail, let out a yelp and whirled to confront him. "Look what you made me do!"

"Me?" He gave her his most innocent expression. "I was just reading your flyer."

"Over my shoulder, and how did I know it was you? You could have been an ax murderer, for heaven's sake." She stuck her thumb between ruby-red lips and sucked gently.

Jeez, he'd have done that for her. He caught his breath, shocked at his own erotic thoughts. "I can't remember the last ax murderer we had in Hard Knox," he said in a choked voice, "but I'm sorry you hurt yourself. Here, let me finish that for you." He reached for the hammer, not the hand.

She held it beyond his reach. "I don't need any help."

"I'd say you do."

"You'd be wrong." Stubbornly she turned back to the task at hand and managed to subdue the nail in a couple of strokes. "There," she said with satisfaction. "That's the last one. Maybe now we'll get some action."

"I hope so," he said without much conviction.

She cocked her head and met his gaze, her own narrow and probing. "I didn't get any response on the ad."

"I'm sorry."

"If this doesn't work..."

He said nothing, just stood there torn in a dozen directions.

She leaned forward, and he could see the determination in her brown eyes. "What's going on, Jack?"

"With what?"

"Why doesn't anyone want to work at the Bar K?"

"I told you, everyone's already got jobs."

"I know what you told me, but I've got a feeling there's a lot more to it than that. Won't you *please* tell me what's going on?"

He wanted to—damn, how he wanted to. But how did you tell a woman that her father had been such an asshole that he had probably forever sullied the name of Keene in Knox County?

The answer was you couldn't, even if you didn't know that the owners of the bigger ranches around here were just circling like sharks, waiting for the sisters to give up and go back where they'd come from.

She sighed and that stubborn little chin rose. "All right, I can see you're not going to help me. Well, I don't need you! I've never needed any man, which is a damn good thing, because no man has ever come through for me."

"Ah, jeez." He couldn't believe what he was hearing. "You're not one of those 'men are no good' types, are you?"

"I sure could be with just about one more little push." She squared her shoulders. "Forget it, okay? Forget we ever had this conversation. Whatever's going on, you're right in the middle of it and I was crazy to think for a single minute that—"

"Now hang on there, you don't know what you're talking about."

"Probably, and you're not going to tell me."

She turned away with disgust so heavy he could feel it.

"Since you're not with me," she announced, "you're against me. I'll just say goodbye and let it go at that."

He watched her walk away, her back straight and her head held high. He wanted to call out to her, run after her, explain everything, but what would be the point? Just because he'd been in her father's debt didn't obligate him to do more than he already had.

She didn't have a clue that he'd been trying like hell to round up a couple of hands for her. But with other ranchers, including the elder Burkes, saying no, the younger Burke saying please didn't go very damn far.

He commiserated with himself on the walk to his pickup. Was it his fault that no one in his right mind was gonna trust anyone named Keene? It really wasn't any of his business anyway, but he did feel kind of protective toward her....

The realization that she'd *hate* that actually made him smile.

FOR THE NEXT twenty-four hours, guilt was Jack's constant companion. Even Petey couldn't shake him out of it. Pa and Grandpa started watching their words as if they thought the least little thing might set him off.

Hell, maybe it would. Maybe until he leveled with Dani he wasn't going to be able to live with himself. But when he set off for the Bar K, he didn't have an idea in the world how he was going to do it.

He pulled into the ranch yard and she came out of the barn to meet him. Despite a cool day, she looked hot and mussed, her hair in tangles around her face, sleeves rolled up, paint splatters all over her.

Lord, she looked good enough to eat. Now he not only didn't know what he was going to say, he'd have to say it with a mouth gone dry.

WHEN SHE SAW HIM drive up, it made her so mad that for a moment she debated whether she should even speak to him. But if she didn't, Toni and Grandma would, and they'd treat him like an honored guest, which he sure as hell wasn't.

So Dani met him halfway, keeping her face carefully blank. "Yes?" she said in a chilly tone.

"Uhh..." He shoved his hands into his jeans pockets and shifted uneasily from one boot to the other. The man looked guilty as sin. "Hired any men yet?"

"You know I haven't."

"Now, I don't know any such thing. For sure." He swallowed hard. "I've been thinking...."

She waited, her head tilted at a challenging angle, refusing to make this easier for him.

After a moment he said, "Maybe a little background is in order here."

"Background on what?"

"On why everybody around here hate—has had a bone to pick with your father."

That got through her icy determination not to respond. "My father?"

"Wil Keene was not... Jeez, this is really hard to say in a nice way." He grimaced. "Wil wasn't too popular is what I'm getting at."

She didn't want to hear this. She'd never known her father, wouldn't know him if he walked up to her right now. She'd grown up despising him for deserting her mother, but if Jack attacked the man, she'd be forced to defend him.

So she said, "I don't want to talk about Wil Keene."

"Maybe not, but he's the reason you're having so much trouble hiring men. He had no friends. Nobody liked him—except for Miss Elsie, of course, and she married him, although no one could ever figure out why."

Dani whirled away. "I said I don't want to hear this."

"Well, you're gonna hear it."

He moved in front of her with such swiftness that she nearly plowed into his chest. He caught her by the upper arms before she could avoid it.

"Folks hereabouts have no reason to feel generous toward Wil Keene or any of his kin. He was a loud-mouthed liar and he'd cheat his own mother if he got the chance."

"Shut up!" He was confirming every rotten opinion she'd ever held about her father, but hearing it was nonetheless painful.

"Maybe you don't know he bragged about his kids. Not until Miss Elsie was gone—until then nobody had any idea he even *had* kids stuck away somewhere else. But after she died, he used to say he had three *just like him*. He'd say, 'You think when I'm gone you'll have everything your own way, but you don't know my kids. *They're just like me.*'"

"As you can plainly see," she said in a voice that shook, "we're *not*."

He nodded. "That's right, *I* can see it, but nobody else has worked up the gumption to get close enough to see much of anything. Yeah, they'll go to the Sorry Bastard to stare at Niki night after night, but that's about the extent of it."

Dani forced a stiff smile that she didn't feel. "I wondered which one of my sisters you were after. So it's Niki, is it? I guess I shouldn't be surprised that—"

His grip on her arms tightened so abruptly that she broke off with a little squeak of surprise. His uneasy expression turned to one of stunned disbelief.

"Niki? Damn, if you believe that—"

And before she knew what he was doing, he yanked her close and kissed her, his mouth taking hers the way a dying man takes water in the desert.

Shocked to the core, she let him have his way with her. And as the furious pressure of his mouth gentled, something cold and tight at the core of her flowered into a molten pool of confusion.

She tingled from head to toe and felt so dizzy that if her arms had been free, she'd have wrapped them around him—just until her head cleared. His tongue touched the tight seam of her lips and she gasped, giving him instant access.

Oh, this was impossible—impossibly lovely. The wildness evaporated and in its wake she tasted a sweetness she'd never before encountered. She didn't know what he was doing, why he was doing it, what he hoped to gain, but she couldn't think straight enough to know how to respond.

He lifted his head at last and looked down at her, his eyes blazing and his breath coming in great gasps. "I'm sorry," he said in a grating voice, "not because I kissed you, but because that's not why I came here today."

Dani's voice again came out a squeak. "Then why did you come here? To insult my father?"

He groaned and his hands fell away from her arms. "I'm sorry about that, but you forced me into it. I was trying to be polite."

It was so much easier to think when he wasn't touching her. "That doesn't answer my question," she managed to say.

"I did *not* come to insult your father."

"I don't care why you *didn't* come, I want to know why you *did* come."

"I...guess you could say I came in response to your ad and those flyers."

She stared at him, suddenly seeing a light at the end of her personal tunnel. "You came about the ad and my flyers?"

He nodded.

She drew in a deep breath and smiled, and this time she meant it. "In that case," she said, "*you're hired!*"

4

SHAKEN, JACK STARED at Dani. "Hang on!" he pleaded. "I didn't come to *respond* to the ad, I came to—"

"You just used that very word—*respond*."

"But I didn't mean it the way you're taking it," he protested, starting to sweat. "I meant respond in the sense of...of *explaining*."

"You can't renege on me now," she cried, her beautiful brown eyes frantic with hope. "I know you've got another job, but the XOX can't possibly need you as much as I—as much as we do."

"Slow down, Dani." Agitated, he lifted his hat to run his fingers through his hair, then clamped the Stetson back on his head. "I didn't intend to mislead you, but you're jumping to all kinds of wrong conclusions."

"After the way you just kissed me—" She caught her breath, her expression open and vulnerable. "Were you just trying to soften me up or...or what? After the way you trashed my father—"

"I didn't trash your father," he objected, feeling the noose tighten. "And he sure as hell didn't have anything to do with my reasons for kissing you."

For a moment she stared at him, then she drew in a deep breath and made a visible effort to steady herself. "You're our last hope," she said in a shaky voice. "I can't believe you've been hanging around just to torment me, but m-maybe that's been your intent all the time." She turned away, head down.

He caught her elbow, which he realized was a major mistake when a tremor of sensual awareness shot up his arm. "I've been hangin' around because I want to help."

"There's only one way you can help." She refused to look at him. "If you come to work here, others will, too."

"It's not that simple."

"Couldn't you come at least for a little while?" She turned those velvet-brown eyes on him. "We're not so bad when you get to know us."

"I never thought—"

"All right." She cut him off. "I can't force you." Shaking off his hand, she turned and continued on toward the house.

He was her last hope and he damn well knew it. He stood that knowledge as long as he could and then called after her. "Okay, you win. I'll come to work at the Bar K, but only temporarily. Is that clearly understood? I'll move my gear into the bunkhouse tomorrow morning."

Not until his last word had died away did she turn to bestow a sparkling smile upon him.

"Oh, *Jack!*"

That was all she said, but he had the distinct impression that if she'd been close enough, she'd have thrown her arms around his neck.

GRANDMA TILLY LOOKED shocked. "You're kidding! Jack's coming to work here?"

"That's right." Dani couldn't conceal her satisfaction.

Grandma finished fluting the piecrust and popped the pan into the oven. "How did you manage that, young lady? I'll bet you had to pull out all the stops."

Dani's smile slipped. "I was desperate. I did what I had to do."

Alarm flared in Grandma's blue eyes. "Danielle Keene, what's that supposed to mean?"

Trying not to be defensive, Dani opened the refrigerator and pulled out a can of soda to buy time. "I guess you could say I kind of...well, I might have manipulated him just a tiny little bit."

"Oh, dear." Grandma's brow wrinkled. "I'm not sure it's a good thing, twisting arms to get cowboys to work here."

"Even if it's the only way?" She wouldn't listen to negative comments after all she'd just gone through. Besides, Jack was the linchpin. Others would follow. "Trust me, Granny," she begged, her confidence restored. "This will work."

Even if Jack did make her powerfully uncomfortable every time he looked at her with that gleam in his eyes. Trying not to think about the kiss, she went humming out the door to find Dobe Whittaker and tell him the good news.

JACK BROKE THE NEWS to his family at supper that night. Grandpa Austin nearly shot up out of his chair.

"You're gonna do *what* for *who?*"

Jack crumbled a biscuit onto his plate. "I'm gonna be helpin' out at the Bar K," he repeated, adding hastily, "just for a little while."

Travis gazed at his son through narrowed eyes. "How long's 'just a little while'?"

"Well..." Jack hated being put on the spot this way. "Most of the summer, I'd guess."

"Most of the—" Austin banged a fist on the table, setting his plate to dancing. "What's got into you, boy? We need you around here."

"I know you do, Grandpa, and I'm sorry. But those women need me worse. The Bar K is all they've got and if somebody doesn't step in they'll lose it sure. Then how would I feel?"

"I know how I'd feel—danged good. They got no business tryin' to run a dude ranch, from what I hear."

Petey rolled a pea across the table. When no one said anything, he rolled another.

Jack's jaw set stubbornly. "You don't know 'em like I do. They're not flighty Eastern women, they're Westerners. They can make a go of this if we give 'em a chance."

Travis snorted. "They're Keenes. 'Nuff said."

In the ensuing silence, everyone went back to plates of fried chicken with all the trimmin's. Except for Jack.

After a moment he said, "I knew you wouldn't like it, but the deed is done. You can hire someone to replace me, but they can't." A sudden thought occurred to him. "You're not puttin' out the word that the Bar K is off-limits, are you? That would be a lowdown dirty trick if you were."

The two older men exchanged quick glances, and Travis said, "So far it hasn't been necessary...in so many words."

"Truth is," Austin admitted, "we want this over and done. We'd give them girls a fair price for that dinky little old ranch, but that lawyer of theirs says they're not interested." He glared at his grandson. "You sweet on one a' them girls already? I can't think of another reason you'd go agin' your own kin this way."

"I'm not going against my own kin," Jack said, ignoring the "sweet on one a' them" observation. "It's your fault I'm in this mess in the first place, Grandpa, since you're the one who had to go get his life saved by the most unpopular man in the county."

"You still on that kick? Wil Keene only done it to—"

A crash interrupted his recitation and they all looked at Petey, angelic while peas rolled over the edge of the table and bounced on the floor. Even before Muriel could charge in with broom in hand, Jack was on his feet and lifting the boy from his chair and onto the floor.

"Com' on, partner. Let's you and me get out of here before we both end up in the doghouse."

"Okay, Uncle Jack." Petey took Jack's hand and they scurried out of the room with Austin's voice pursuing them: "This ain't finished yet by a long shot!"

It was, as far as Jack was concerned.

JACK MOVED INTO the Bar K bunkhouse the next morning, under Dobe's approving eye.

"I thought Dani was joshin' me when she said you was comin', but here you are," the old cowboy drawled.

"To tell you the truth, I kinda got roped into it." Jack stowed his war bag under a lower bunk. "So bring me up to date. How's everything going?"

"Better than I would have expected," Dobe admitted. "These women ain't half-bad. They're all workers, that's for sure. Toni and the old lady are getting the house squared away and Dani works right alongside me. We've got the barn in pretty decent shape, except for a few shingles still missin' on the roof. Dani said today she'll climb up there and—"

"Like hell." Jack straightened abruptly. "She'd fall and break her fool neck. I'll do it."

Dobe beamed. "Worried about her neck, are you? It's a mighty pretty neck if you go for that kinda thing."

"Yeah, well..." Jack turned toward the door. "We're burnin' daylight, old-timer."

Dobe followed him out into the sunshine. "Even with you here, we're still shorthanded. I swear, I don't know what it'll take for folks to get over that Wil Keene. You reckon you might put in a good word for these gals?"

Jack gave a disgusted grunt. "Yeah, I reckon I might do that, but don't say anything. I don't want to get anyone's hopes up prematurely."

As it turned out, nothing needed to be said. Dani's hopes were sky-high without anyone uttering a word. Jack realized how high when the dinner bell pealed and they all sat down together at the small table in the kitchen.

Dani passed the big bowl of chicken and dumplings, bestowing a smile along with the food. "I can't believe how much we all accomplished today," she said enthusiastically. "Why, at this rate—"

"Don't get too carried away," Jack warned. "The barn is only the first part of it. We still have to work our way through all the other outbuildings and then we've got fences and equipment to mend and stock to sort and evaluate."

"Whew!" Grandma smiled. "Makes me tired just listening to all that."

"Not as tired as it makes us to do it," Dobe retorted, his voice and expression as hostile as if he'd been personally attacked.

"Well, my goodness," Granny protested, "don't yell at me!"

"Not yellin'," Dobe declared sullenly. "Just statin' facts. There's too much work for only two men if you expect to have this place ready for the first dudes in April."

Toni looked anxiously around the table. "Heaven knows, we've tried to hire the help we need. For some reason, no one will even talk to us about working here."

"They will now," Dani said.

Jack's heart dropped to the vicinity of his stomach. "Now, Dani, don't go gettin' all—"

"Jack, you know it's true. Everybody in the country seems to be your friend. I'm sure if you...you know, just kind of pass the word that we're not *complete* idiots..." She grinned suddenly, her brown eyes sparkling. "Stretch the point if you have to."

He couldn't resist returning her smile, however reluctantly. "I might have to."

She laughed out loud. "Whatever it takes, Jack. Whatever it takes..."

WITH THE BARN ROOF repaired, the men spent the next three days fixing fences, a job that was never truly done on a ranch. Between animals both wild and domesticated, fences were always busted or down or in the wrong place. And the fences on the Bar K were worse than most, further testament to neglect.

But the weather was warming and grass was

greening and birds were singing. Jack was getting jumpier and touchier by the hour, eventually leading him to suspect a serious case of spring fever.

Then he rode his horse into the ranch yard at the end of one long, hard day and saw a sight that made his gut clench and his breath rasp in his throat.

Dani, up on Sundance...concentrating totally on the Appaloosa while she put him through the kind of paces Jack had only seen in old cowboy movies. The horse danced lightly to the left, reversed the procedure to the right, then bowed until his muzzle touched his leg. Throughout the entire sequence, Jack never saw Dani so much as move a muscle.

Riding out of his hiding place around the corner of the barn, he could see he'd startled her. Nevertheless, she smiled and waved before hopping off the speckled horse. Waiting for Jack to approach, she slipped an arm across the proudly arched neck.

"Damn," he said admiringly, "that was *good*. Did you teach him all that yourself?"

"I'm not sure who taught who." She rubbed the horse's velvety nose, her voice soft when she spoke about the Appy. "We kind of learned it together."

Jack swung out of the saddle. "Where'd you get old Sundance, anyway?"

"He was a gift from my boss. I worked at the Box W before we came here. Maybe you've heard of it?"

"Yeah, I think I have." He should go put away his horse and yet he lingered, thinking he'd never seen

Dani so relaxed and at ease. "What did you do at the Box W?"

"Bookkeeper officially, but you know how it is at a ranch. During emergencies, I did just about everything." She gave him a quick, warm smile. "Sundance was my reward. He was an orphan and nobody had time to mess with him anyway, so you could say I raised him. We've been great pals ever since."

That rapport was obvious. "Has he got any more tricks?"

"Lots of 'em. I thought maybe he and I could do a little show for the guests sometime. Toni does rope tricks and Niki is a terrific mistress of ceremonies." Dani looked at him with an expression so open and trusting that it shocked him. "What do you think?"

"I think the dudes would love it." *Hell, I'd love it.* "Want me to put Sundance in the corral for you? I'm about to—"

"Dani!"

They glanced around to find Toni hurrying toward them, her expression filled with concern.

"What is it?" Dani asked.

"I found another one of those blasted notes." Toni held out a piece of paper, her exasperation clear. "Honestly, why is he doing this?"

"Who's doing what?" Jack inquired.

"Wil Keene—our father." Dani unfolded the torn scrap and read, "Earn your keep, little girls. This is no free lunch." She added a gratuitous, "Good grief, what's that supposed to mean?"

"I don't know," Toni said indignantly, "but I don't like it. It's...it's insulting is what it is."

"How many have you found?" Jack asked, intrigued in spite of himself.

Dani shrugged. "Four or five, wouldn't you say, Toni? And none of them make any sense. Like we're not working like dogs here? The man must have been a sadist!"

"You should know," Jack agreed mildly, and was surprised by the way Dani caught her breath.

"What exactly do you mean by that?"

He blinked. "Just what it sounds like. He was *your* father."

"That doesn't mean—" She bit off hot words. "Never mind. This one will go into the round file with all the others." The suddenly bright expression on her face was at odds with her obvious annoyance. "Is it suppertime, Toni?"

"Just about. Grandma will be ringing the bell any minute." She turned back toward the house. "Niki's at work so it'll just be the five of us tonight."

As far as Jack was concerned, that was still three too many.

JACK PUSHED AWAY from the table with a sigh of satisfaction. "Mrs. Collins, that was, beyond a doubt, the best lemon pie I ever ate." He patted his checkered shirt for emphasis.

The old lady beamed. "Thank you kindly. I *do* get a good response with that recipe."

Jack nodded. "One thing's for sure, your guests are gonna eat high off the hog."

"Our guests," Dani declared, "will have more than good food. Right, Toni?"

"Right!" Toni began to gather dishes from the table. "They'll have a great time or we'll all die trying."

Jack stacked his own dishes and glanced at Dobe, but the old cowboy was still shoveling in the pie. Then his gaze touched Dani's and held.

He smiled and her expression turned wary. Undeterred, he said, "I have to go by the XOX to pick up some stuff and then I thought I'd drop into the Sorry Bastard. Want to tag along?"

She stiffened still more. "No, thanks." She put all her attention on the stacking.

"It won't take long," he coaxed. "Don't you want to see how Niki's doing at her new job?"

"No, but apparently you do." Dani stood, picked up the stack of dishes and carried them to the counter near the sink.

While Jack tried to digest her sharp retort. She thought he just wanted to see Niki? Hell, Niki wasn't the Keene who set his pulse to pounding.

She bustled back over, taking obvious pains not to look at him. He watched her for a moment, then said, "I think you've got the wrong idea, here. I want to drop in at the saloon to—" See if he could twist any arms to get riders for the Bar K.

But he didn't get to say that because she cut him off.

"I understand perfectly. Have a good time." And she spun around and headed into the pantry.

Well, hell. He glanced at Toni. "How about you? Would you like to go into town with me?"

"You know, I'd love to, but I was in the middle of a job I have to finish tonight." She did, indeed, look regretful. "It's the public bathroom off the great room. The paint should be dry by now and I have to move stuff back in."

"If you need any help, I'd be glad to—"

"No, no, you've worked hard all day." She shooed him off. "You run along and give Niki my best."

"I'll do that." Damn, he'd have liked to put Dani in her place by escorting her sister, but likable as Toni was, having her along was not what he really wanted. "In that case, I'll see y'all tomorrow."

He walked out of the room with Dobe at his heels, just as Dani walked back in.

Toni gave a regretful sigh. "That would have been fun," she said.

"What would have?" Dani asked, relieved to see the last of Jack for another day.

"Going into town with Jack." Toni's mouth stretched in a big grin. "He's not only a top hand, he's a really cute guy. I mention this in case you haven't noticed."

Dani sniffed disdainfully, determined to hide her reaction to Toni's revelation. Apparently Jack didn't care *which* Keene sister he squired around. "All I've noticed is that he's good at his job," she said airily. "Believe me, that's all I'm interested in."

Toni's good humor slipped. "Ohh, Dani, you make me so mad sometimes! You can't see the forest for the trees. Just because one guy treated you bad doesn't mean—"

"That's not why. Toni, you are *so* naive. If you think Jack's such a hunk, why don't *you* go after him? You always said you wanted to marry a cowboy and now one's dropped into your lap."

"I might, if he ever looked at me the way he—"

"Girls, girls." Grandma, who'd been openly listening, shook her silvery head. "Please don't squabble. You know it gives me a headache."

"Sorry, Granny." Toni gave the little lady a quick hug. "But we weren't squabbling, we were *discussing*." She winked at her sister. "I just hope you come to your senses one of these days."

Dani rolled her eyes toward the ceiling. It was one of her senses—the one called horse sense—that warned her not to let Jack get under her skin. And it wasn't because of that rotten experience with her boss's son, either. It was because everything in her cried out for her to fall into his arms like a ripe peach.

Anything she wanted that bad couldn't possibly be good for her.

PA WAS WORKING ON the books and Grandpa was peering over the rims of half-glasses at a newspaper when Jack walked in. They greeted him with word-less grunts—recognition, nothing more.

"I'm glad you're both here," Jack announced. "That way I'll only have to say this once."

Travis put down his pen, his expression brimming with suspicion. "Say what?"

"The Bar K is in bad need of a couple of men and I'm gonna see who I can entice over there."

Austin wadded up his newspaper and tossed it aside. "You sayin' you're gonna steal XOX men? I won't have it, Jack!"

"*Steal*'s the wrong word, Grandpa." Jack had thought about this long and hard and was prepared. "Think of it more like *borrowing*. The XOX is overstaffed at the moment anyway, considering that we'd already agreed to pull back on the dude operation and concentrate more on the cattle and eXOXtic animals."

"That don't give you any right to—"

"Hang on, Pa." Travis tapped pen against paper. "Jack, what are you really up to?"

Jack felt a surprised flush heat his face. "Nothin', not a dad-gummed thing."

"I don't believe you. You been hoverin' over those women like—hell, like their trained lapdog."

"That's a damned lie," Jack blustered. "You know why I'm helpin' 'em out—because Grandpa had to go get himself saved by their daddy."

"Don't go blamin' me," Austin hollered. "I didn't ask Keene to pull me outa that truck." He glared over his newspaper. "Besides, you've paid him and them girls back a dozen times over."

Travis said, "Calm down, Pa. That's not the reason, anyway." He peered at his only surviving son with narrowed eyes. "Which one is it, Jack? The one workin' at the Bastard is a real knockout."

Jack spun around toward the door. "I don't have to take this," he snapped. "I just don't want either one of you gettin' all worked up if a couple of XOX men take a...let's call it a leave of absence."

"Let's call it treason!" Austin yelled after his grandson. "Let's call it—" But Jack was gone so the old man subsided, grumbling, "Women!"

"That's what it is, all right." Travis shoved back his chair so he could stretch out his long legs. "He's sweet on one of those Keene sisters, sure as shootin'."

Austin scowled at his son. "So far he's been smarter than the rest of the Burke men," he announced. "By the time I was his age I'd already been married and divorced and so had you."

"Don't say it like you're proud of it," Travis retorted.

Austin bristled. "What I'm proud of is the fact that us Burke men finally caught on. We're gettin' along just fine with no women—well, no women unless you count Muriel, and I don't. She's just the housekeeper and baby-sitter, is all."

"Well, one a' the Keenes has got her spurs in Jack and you can bank on it."

Both men subsided into gloomy introspection. After a while, Austin said, "Well, hell, what we gonna do about this?"

JACK WAS SURPRISED to find a lively crowd in the Sorry Bastard—at least, lively for a weeknight. Spotting several XOX cowboys, he joined them at their table.

Niki appeared almost immediately. In jeans and a plaid shirt open at the throat, she looked as if she'd just stepped off the pages of some sexy magazine. She wasn't as good-looking as Dani, but she was still fine.

"Draft beer," Jack said, thinking about the best way to approach the three cowboys watching the barmaid so avidly.

"Coming right up." With a friendly smile, she turned away.

"Fellas," Jack began, then ceased speaking abruptly because he realized no one was paying him the least attention. All three were staring after Niki with lovesick expressions.

"Man, that is one good-lookin' babe," Dylan Sawyer breathed.

"Oh, yeah." That was Joe Bob Muskowitz agreeing.

Manuel Reyes said, "*Sí!*" and rolled dark eyes. "Too bad she's a—"

"Don't even say it."

Now Jack had their attention, scandalized though it might be.

Dylan frowned. "But that's what we always say— too bad they're Keenes."

"Yeah," Joe Bob agreed. "Hating Keenes has been a

civic duty around here for years." He sighed. "It's gettin' hard, though—damned hard."

"Then don't do it," Jack said, fed up with the lot of them. "You come in here and moon over Niki Keene and drop more money on tips than you spend on beer, but you still act like the lot of them's contaminated or something."

"Hell, shoot, what's *your* problem?" Joe Bob demanded.

"It's not my problem, it's—"

"Here you go, Jack." Niki set a frosty mug before him with another friendly smile. "So how're things at home?"

"At home?" Miguel stared at his boss's son.

"The Bar K," Niki supplied. "Didn't you know Jack's working there now?" With a wink that included them all, she sashayed away, leaving Jack to face his moment of truth.

5

"I WAS ABOUT TO MENTION that," Jack protested. "I've only been workin' at the Bar K for a few days and—".

"A *Burke* working for a *Keene*?" Dylan looked at the other two cowboys for support. "Now I've heard everything. Does your pa know about this?"

"What do you think, I've kept it a secret?" Disgusted with this turn of events, Jack picked up his beer and swallowed a big gulp. This wasn't going quite the way he'd planned. The three XOX hands were obviously scandalized. "Look," he said abruptly, "here's the deal...."

And he started talking fast enough to keep any of them from getting a word in edgewise.

DANI WAS STANDING beneath a light post beside the corral, peering into the darkness, when Jack drove his pickup all the way to the front of the bunkhouse. Since he would obviously see her, she decided to simply brazen it out if forced to do so.

Which, of course, she was when he climbed out of the cab and came toward her instead of disappearing into the bunkhouse.

"What's up?" he asked, halting before her.

She kept her gaze anywhere but on him. "I heard a commotion and came to see what was causing it."

"Commotion?"

"Dogs barking, horses running—that kind of commotion."

"Want me to go look?"

"No need. Everything seems to have settled down."

For a few moments they stood there in silence, close but not touching. Dani felt the pulse pounding in her throat and tried to ignore it, along with her curiosity about his trip to the Sorry Bastard.

"Niki says hi," he announced suddenly.

"Oh." What was there to say? She and Niki lived in the same house, after all, so she didn't expect any news flashes. She licked her lips. "Anything going on in town?"

"Nah, not really."

Silence again. She should walk away, go back into the house and leave him standing here all alone, but somehow she felt rooted to the spot. And then her errant thoughts turned in directions she'd rather they not go.

Had she focused her frustration with all things Texan on him? He was, as Toni had said, a top hand. With his skills, he could get a job anywhere—he'd been working at the XOX, for goodness sakes, one of the biggest operations in Texas. She was lucky to have him, even if she'd had to do a number to get him.

She turned toward him now and said brightly, "You didn't happen to hire us any cowboys while you were in town, did you?"

He sighed. "I tried," he admitted. "Maybe after they have a little time to think about it..."

"Thanks for trying." Dani gritted her teeth. After a moment, she said, "Y'know, I'm starting to take this personally."

"Don't." He shifted his feet as if uncomfortable. "I told you, everyone who wants a job already has one."

"There's more to it than that."

He seemed to stiffen. "Such as?"

"I've been nosing around," she said slowly. "It's obvious that no one in Hard Knox likes us—or maybe I should say, no one *trusts* us. It's got to be more than just bad feelings toward our father."

"You, uh, know...uh, you know how it is in small towns," he hemmed and hawed. "People carry grudges...."

"Yes, but there's got to be more to it than that. For one thing, I suspect that the bigger, more powerful dude ranches are actively working against us."

"Ah, come on, Dani, are you talking sabotage?" He sounded incredulous. "This little pip-squeak out-fit—" He stopped short. "I'm sorry, I didn't mean to insult the Bar K."

"That's all right. I don't suppose it's any secret that we're operating on a shoestring. We may not be exactly big-time but the Bar K does have a long and, as far as I could discover, honorable history."

"Yeah, sure it does."

"Maybe the biggies just want to flick us away like...like a fly. The fact that no one will work for us is just the tip of the iceberg. No one's even got a kind word for us."

"It's nothing personal, honest." He looked desperate for her to believe him—too desperate. "Trust me on that."

"I don't know that I can when—"

"I said *trust me*." He spun her around into his arms and kissed her.

She'd been there before and knew how dangerous it could be to her mental and emotional health. She'd yank herself free, probably slap his face and berate him soundly...just as soon as she could pull herself together.

In the meantime, she'd return his kiss, let her lips part just enough, let him curve his hand around her bottom and haul her hard against the long lean length of him....

She was losing it. *Act!*

With a mighty shove, she was out of his arms and facing him with fire in her belly and her heart. "What are you *doing?*" she cried. "You can't just grab me anytime you feel like it and—"

"If I grabbed you every time I felt like it, neither one of us would get much else done," he growled. "Jeez!" He shoved his hat back on his head, dark hair spilling over his forehead. "That's one reason you're having trouble fittin' in around here—you're so danged touchy!"

Touchy? He'd called her *touchy*? She watched him stalk over to the bunkhouse, thinking that he didn't know what touchy was, but she just might show him one of these days.

BY NOON THE NEXT DAY, Dani still hadn't found an opportunity to cut Jack dead with the icy disdain she'd chosen as her best course of action, because she hadn't even seen him. At lunch she ventured to inquire about his continuing absence.

Grandma looked surprised. "He's got the day off. Didn't you know?"

"I didn't give him the day off. What does he think he's doing, just walking off anytime he—"

"*I* gave it to him," Toni interrupted calmly. "Why not? He's been working like a dog ever since he got here."

That, Dani acknowledged to herself grudgingly, was the truth. Still, she couldn't let it go. "He could have at least talked to *me* about it," she grumbled.

"That's true," Toni said too sweetly. "I guess he was under the impression that I was one of the bosses of this outfit, too."

"Oh, Toni, I'm sorry!" Dani meant it. "Sometimes I just get so carried away that I forget we're all in this together."

"We certainly are," Toni agreed, but she softened her words with a smile. "I'm perfectly happy to let you be the boss, but once in a while I see something that needs doing and I just do it. That was one of them. When Jack said he had personal business to tend to, I said sure. Which is exactly what you'd have said."

Probably, Dani thought, but first she'd have asked what that "personal" business was—*oh, bite your tongue,* she scolded herself. Jack's personal business was none of hers.

Granny leaned forward. "Would one of you girls have time to do some shopping for me this afternoon? I've got a whole list of stuff I need from the grocery and hardware stores."

"Not me." Toni shook her head. "I'm starting work on the cabins this afternoon. Dani?"

Dani sighed. "Sure, I can do it." Why not? Jack wasn't around to keep her on her mettle so she might as well.

"I DON'T KNOW WHAT SIZE," Dani said. "Just nails. See?" She offered Grandma's handwritten list and there it was, the word *nails* written in a fine and graceful hand.

The hardware clerk peered closely at the piece of paper, as if he could glean a clue. He frowned. "What're they for?" He tried another tack. "Hanging pictures or attaching shingles?"

Dani laughed. "Well, I don't think she's planning on going up on the roof, so shingles are probably out.

She could be hanging pictures or—you know, just minor repair stuff. Granny doesn't do fine carpentry."

"You could call her and ask," the clerk suggested, his expression disapproving. Apparently to him, nails were sacred. "I wouldn't want to sell you the wrong thing."

"Believe me, if you do I won't blame you. There's really no reason to bother her with this. Don't you have, like...an assortment?"

"That's doable."

Smothering her smile, Dani followed him down the aisle into the interior of the store. Spotting a display of hooks, she hesitated. She could use a few of those in her bedroom.

"*Ooof!*" With her gaze on the display, she'd managed to walk right into someone, a very short someone.

"Hey, lady!"

Small hands shoved at her, and she looked down to find a freckle-faced boy of perhaps four staring at her with a wrinkled brow and an out-thrust lower lip.

"I beg your pardon!" She smiled at his offended expression. "Did I hurt you?"

"Nah," the boy scoffed, his chest puffing out beneath his striped T-shirt. "I'm tough!"

"And a good thing, too. I guess I wasn't paying much attention to where I was going."

"That's okay," the boy said. "You're a *girl*."

Startled, she recognized scorn in his tone—and for one so young it just didn't seem right. "Being a girl's not so bad," she objected. "I've been one all my life and—"

"*Petey!*"

The kid started and glanced over his shoulder as if fully prepared to run—away from, not toward, the accusing voice. Before he could make his getaway, Dani grabbed him by a hand.

"Take it easy," she soothed. "Somebody's looking for you and—"

That somebody was Jack, skidding around the end of the row and stopping short at sight of the two of them. "Dad-gummit, Petey, how come you take off every time I turn my back?"

"'Cause it's fun when you chase me!" The boy struggled mightily, but this time it was to run toward the man, not away.

Dani turned him loose and he did just that. Startled and disconcerted, she watched the kid wrap his arms around the man's legs in a mighty hug. Who *was* this child? Could he possibly be…Jack's *son?*

The same Jack who was grinning at her, saying, "Hi, Dani. I didn't expect to run into you today."

"Obviously." She lifted her chin, outraged that he'd kept something so important from her. If there was one thing she couldn't stand, it was a secretive man. "If you'll excuse me, I have to go pay for some nails."

He spoke coaxingly. "What's your hurry? Don't you want to meet Petey?"

"I already have." Clenching her jaw, she turned away.

"But—"

"Uncle Jack, why's that lady mad?"

At the boy's high-pitched inquiry, Dani stopped short. *Uncle* Jack! How wonderful! She turned with a smile.

"Aha!" Jack said, his hazel eyes gleaming. "You thought Petey was mine. Admit it."

"I *am* yours, Uncle Jack!" Petey laughed up at the tall man, adding, "Can I have a quarter?"

"Sure." Jack dug around in his pocket for change, his amused glance never leaving Dani. "Here you go, kid." He dumped a handful of coins into the outstretched hand.

"Thanks!" Petey rushed toward the front of the store and the gum ball machines stationed just inside the door.

Dani smiled after him. "He's cute."

"Yeah. He's also a handful, but don't change the subject. You thought he was mine, didn't you?"

"I...thought there was a very good possibility."

"I don't have any children, Dani."

"Since you're not married, that works out very well," she said lightly, denying even to herself the relief she felt. "If you'll excuse me, I have to get those nails now."

"Okay." He hesitated before adding, "Then maybe you'd care to join me and Petey for ice cream at the Dairy Dew."

"You know," she said slowly, "I think I'd like that. I'll be right with you."

Moving to the register, she smiled happily to herself as she paid for Granny's nails. She liked children, but she wouldn't have liked discovering that Jack had one of his own. A nephew...now, that was perfectly acceptable.

PETEY PROMPTLY DIVED into his ice cream cone with such a vengeance that the hard chocolate coating cracked and fell on the floor. Jack groaned and reached for a handful of napkins.

"Petey, how many times do I have to tell you—"

"Here," Dani said, "I'll do that. You get the boy some more chocolate."

"Yeah," Petey echoed, "more chocolate, Uncle Jack!" He thrust out his denuded white cone.

By the time Jack got back to the table with the newly chocolatized cone, Dani had cleaned up the mess and was giggling with the boy. It gave Jack a good feeling to see them this way.

She tasted a spoonful of strawberry ice cream and sighed blissfully. "This is really good," she said. The tip of her pink tongue darted out to lick her lips, and Jack's mouth went dry. "Petey tells me he lives with you."

"That's right." Jack could barely taste his ice cream.

She frowned. "But you're staying at the Bar K now."

"My grandpa and our housekeeper do most of the

baby-sitting," Jack explained. "It'll be easier next year when the kid goes to kindergarten."

"I'm smart," Petey offered. "I can read and stuff."

"Really?" Her eyes widened and her glance flew to Jack, who rolled *his* eyes and shook his head. She grinned and turned back to the boy. "I could tell you were smart. You'll have to read to me someday."

"I can," Petey declared in that same absolutely certain way kids have with everything up to and including dinosaur sightings.

"I believe you," she said. "Y'know, Petey, you should have your uncle bring you to visit me one of these days. Would you like that?"

"I dunno," he said, watching her round-eyed. "Why?"

"Why, because I like you, that's all. We'll be refilling the swimming pool any day and we could swim—"

"I got one a' them," he interrupted.

"Oh. Well, we could go riding...."

"On horses? I got one a' them, too."

"I see." She bit her lip to keep from laughing, obviously believing that these claims were just about as valid as the one about reading. "Isn't there anything...?"

"I got no time for wimmin!" Petey swallowed the last of his ice-cream cone and looked expectantly at his uncle. "Can I go home now?"

"What's your hurry?" Jack had been enjoying the

little exchange between the two of them. "Relax and—"

"Not on my account." Dani put her spoon on the table beside the paper cup that had held ice cream. "I've got to get a move on." She offered her hand to Petey. "It was delightful meeting you."

"Huh?" Petey blinked, then stuck out his pudgy hand.

"And you..." Her amused glance sought Jack. "They say that anyone who's loved by kids and dogs can't be all bad. Maybe I've misjudged you, after all."

"I've been trying to tell you that," he said with a faint smile. "I should have thought of softening you up with the kid sooner."

Their glances met and held like magnets. He saw her brown eyes widen, heard the soft intake of her breath—

"Hey, Jack!"

Three cowboys—Dylan, Joe Bob and Miguel—plunged through the door of the Dairy Dew and came to a stop beside the small round table, where they stood shoulder to shoulder. Jack blinked and tried to get back to the present moment.

"You lookin' for me?" he inquired.

"Well," Dylan said, "no. As a matter of fact, we're lookin' for her."

"Me?" Dani's big brown eyes got even bigger.

"You still lookin' for hands?" Joe Bob asked.

"Y-yes." Hope leaped into her expression.

"Then here we are," Miguel declared, "best darn vaqueros in Texas, at your service, ma'am."

"Oh, my gosh! Do you mean it?" Dani sprang to her feet. "I mean, you'll work for me and my sisters at the Bar K? The *Keene* sisters?"

"Yep," Dylan said, "that's what we mean. You want us, we're yours."

She wanted them, all right. Jack figured anyone could see that, and he didn't like the prickle of resentment that streaked up his spine. He was sure she only wanted them to *work* on the Bar K, and yet the gratitude in her glance made him wonder....

Damnation, this was what he got for meddling. He almost wished he'd never gone on that arm-twisting campaign.

Jealousy, he realized, was not a pretty emotion.

ONCE THE THREE NEW cowboys were on board, work proceeded at a breakneck pace. It was all Dani could do to keep ahead of them with the schedule of repairs and improvements.

Her biggest problem now was the stock—or lack of it. She might be able to fake it with a handful of longhorns for atmosphere, but she was shy at least a half-dozen horses. And they had to be gentle horses, safe for dudes to ride. Where she'd come up with the money to pay for them even if she found them she couldn't imagine—

"Dani!"

She looked up from her ledgers to find Toni hurrying toward her, waving a piece of paper. "I've found another one," she declared, placing the paper on the desk with a thump.

Dani read, "Elsie's trunk a keeper." She frowned. "What do you suppose *that* means?"

"Who cares?" Toni looked wild-eyed. "This is driving me crazy, Dani, all these goofy notes. Why did he do it? It's not *nice!*"

"From what I've heard, he wasn't a very nice man." Dani's lips tightened. "But then, we knew that."

"No, we *don't* know that," Toni said, lifting her chin stubbornly. "He must have had a few good qualities. Don't forget, we only know Grandma's side of it."

"Grandma's side is good enough for me. Wil Keene went into Elk Tooth and sweet-talked a young girl out of her money and her...her *virtue.* Then he took said money and said virtue and hightailed it out of town one jump ahead of the posse."

"Mama wouldn't have pressed charges," Toni said. "She wasn't like that."

"Maybe not," Dani retorted, "but in her shoes, I sure would have. And she finally divorced him, so she'd obviously given up on him. As far as I'm concerned, we can take all those notes and—"

A knock on the door interrupted her outburst, and the sisters looked at each other in consternation. The ranch was so far from town that casual guests were unusual, to say the least.

But not unwelcome. Toni hurried to open the door, a smile on her face. A stranger stood there.

"Have I the honor of addressing two of the Misses Keene?" the courtly looking gentleman inquired pleasantly, glancing from one sister to the other.

Toni smiled. "That's right. I'm Toni and that's my sister, Dani."

"Delighted to make your acquaintance." The man doffed his hat—*not* a cowboy hat—and bowed from the waist. "I'm Stanley Wexler of Hard Knox Realty. I've come to make you ladies an offer I hope you won't be able to refuse."

"Realty?" Toni frowned and glanced at her sister. "I don't understand."

Dani's stomach clenched into a knot. "I do." She stepped forward. "Somebody wants to buy the Bar K."

"They do, indeed. May I come in and tell you about it?"

"Of course." Toni stepped aside, gesturing for the man to enter.

"Hold it right there!" Dani's order stopped the man in his tracks. "Not to be rude or anything, but you're wasting your time. The ranch is not for sale."

Stanley Wexler smiled disarmingly. "You haven't heard the offer yet. My client has instructed me to—"

"It doesn't matter," Dani said quickly. "We won't sell at *any* price."

The real estate agent's smile didn't slip. He looked

at Toni. "May I assume your sister speaks for you as well?"

"Of course." But Toni seemed more puzzled than assured.

Mr. Wexler looked annoyed. "In that case, I must apologize for wasting your time. It's just that my clients have had their eye on this property for some time."

"Who *are* your clients?" Dani asked casually, sure that whoever it was must be behind the drive to undermine efforts to revive the ranch.

"The gentlemen of the XOX," Wexler said. "If you were concerned that it wasn't a good faith offer or that the prospective buyers wouldn't have the wherewithal to support such a purchase, I'm sure you now realize that is not the case." He looked at them, hopeful again.

The XOX, Dani thought. *Now I know who my enemy is.* It would be easy enough for such a high-stakes player in the local economy to put out the word: "Don't give the Bar K an even break. Wear the new owners down and they'll be glad to sell out."

"I was just curious," she said to Wexler. "The ranch isn't for sale, not to anyone at any price. Feel free to quote me."

"Yes, ma'am, I'll surely do that. If you change your mind..." He offered his business card and Toni took it. "Good day to you both, then."

The sisters stood silently by while he climbed into his big shiny car and drove away. Then Dani took the business card, stared at it for a moment and stuffed it into her jeans pocket.

"I've got to get out to the barn," she said shortly. "If you need me, holler."

"Okay." Toni bit her lip. "Don't you think maybe we should have at least listened to him? He was a nice man, Dani."

"He didn't come here to be our friend, he came here to take our home away from us."

"But—"

"The XOX, Toni. Remember it. Because that's the enemy."

DANI STOMPED TOWARD the barn looking mad enough to kick a cow dog. Jack, unsaddling his horse near the tack room in the shade of cottonwood trees, decided to let Dobe handle this one. Jack had more important things on his mind.

Like calling off his father and grandfather, who seemed determined to kick up a ruckus with these new owners of the Bar K. Jack didn't like walking such a fine line between family and duty. Turning the bay loose into the pasture, he gave the animal a pat on the backside to send him on his way. Turning, he saw Dobe ambling over, shaking his grizzled head with every step.

Jack stifled a groan. "Now what?" Seemed like it was always something.

Dobe came to a halt in a puff of dust. "That woman would drive a wooden man crazy," he announced.

"Anything in particular got her riled this time?"

"Stan Wexler just tried to make an offer on the ranch. She wouldn't even listen to it, though—sent him packing, I gather."

Jack's blood ran cold. "Who—?"

"She didn't say. I got the feelin' it didn't matter a whole helluva lot *who* it was, she'd be just as mad."

It mattered to Jack—a lot. "Look," he said brusquely, "there's something I gotta do. I'll be back as soon as I can."

Dobe nodded. "Yeah, sure, go on and leave me with a woman on the warpath. What d'you care?"

Unfortunately, Jack cared plenty, but first he had to find out if his suspicions were true.

"DID YOU SEND STAN WEXLER over to make an offer on the Bar K?"

Austin's lower lip thrust out challengingly. "Yep."

"Dammit, Grandpa, I thought I told you—"

"You young pup! Since when do you tell your elders what they can and can't do?"

"When they're fixin' to go off half-cocked!" Jack shoved his hands through his hair distractedly. "All you've managed to do is get Dani riled up again. Your chances of getting that place were slim before, but now they're none."

"Dani, is it?" The old man's eyes narrowed craftily. "I been wonderin' which one of them wimmin had you purring like a lap cat, and now I guess I know."

"You don't know sic 'em!" But he did, and Jack realized that he'd given himself away. "You really blew it," he said shortly. "The next time you get any bright ideas about the Bar K, can you at least check 'em with me first?"

"Why? So you can run over there and tell the enemy?" Austin's lip curled. "Whose side are you on, anyway? Is blood still thicker than water or are you a turnin' agin your own?"

Jack saw red. It took a full minute for him to get hold of himself enough to speak. "Grandpa," he said, carefully enunciating every syllable, "if anyone else said that to me I'd beat the holy sh—"

"Uncle Jack!" Petey bounced into the room astride his stick horse, Rover. "Did you come home to play with me?"

Jack gritted his teeth. "Later, I promise. Now I got something I have to do."

"WHAT DO YOU MEAN, Jack had errands?" Still in a bad mood, Dani glared at Dobe.

The old cowboy shrugged, completely immune to her displeasure. "The boy's got another life, after all."

"Not while I'm paying his wages, he doesn't."

Dobe scoffed. "Like he needs your wages."

Dani blinked. "What's that supposed to mean? Of course he does. Everybody needs a paycheck."

"Not if they're in line to inherit the biggest ranch in this part of Texas, they don't," he retorted. "I'd advise you to be a whole lot nicer if you want to keep him, missy."

"The biggest..." She stared at him, aghast. "You don't mean...?"

"Don't mean what? What ya gettin' at?"

She swallowed hard. "You don't mean Jack wasn't just working at the XOX, do you?"

"Working at it! Hell, the Burkes has owned it since there *was* an XOX. Old Austin's my age or better. Then there's his boy Travis, and Travis's boy Jack, and Petey—his folks is dead, you know."

"Jack's *family* owns the XOX?" She was having an awful time taking it in. "Then why did he come to work for *me*?"

Dobe cracked a grin that just kept getting bigger. "I'd say that's as plain as the nose on your face," he drawled.

She nodded slowly. "You just could be right about that," she said in a low voice, thinking words like *spy* and *double-dealer* and *back-stabber*.

And one more: *revenge!*

6

"SUPPERTIME!" Grandma Tilly sang out.

Crossing to the house from the barn where he'd parked his pickup, Jack increased his speed. He had the feeling that time was of the essence if he was going to calm Dani down enough to listen to what he had to say in defense of his indefensible elders.

By the time he reached the back door, Tilly had disappeared inside. Filled with foreboding, he followed.

Everyone else was already at the table: Tilly and Toni, Dobe and the three cowboys, and Dani, who looked up with dangerously narrowed eyes.

She was holding it against him personally, he knew in a flash. His own temper rising, he pulled out his chair and sat down.

Tilly looked around the table, her blue eyes wide with apprehension just before they closed in prayer. "For what we are about to receive, O Lord, we thank you." She hesitated before adding, "And we ask you to help us to remember to be *nice* to each other. Amen."

"Amen!" Dylan echoed, a big grin spreading across his face. "I swear, these are the best eats I *ever* had. Grandma Tilly, you're the best."

Her dimples flashed. "Thank you kindly, young man."

"Humph!" Dobe's lip curled. "Quit talkin' and pass the pork chops, somebody."

The platter moved from hand to hand around the table, each diner helping him or herself before passing it on. All except Dani, who just handed it curtly to Dobe.

Tilly, unfortunately, noticed. "What's the matter, dear? Don't you feel well?"

"I'm all right," Dani said stiffly.

The platter reached Jack. Finding himself completely without appetite, he set it on the table before him.

Tilly the hawk was still on the job. "You, too, Jack? My goodness, I hope there's nothing going around that's catching!"

"I doubt it," he muttered, feeling foolish to be sitting at a table with an empty plate, but too apprehensive to rectify it. What was Dani so bent out of shape for? Surely she didn't think that he—! He stared at her, comprehension dawning. She *did* think he'd conspired against her.

Abruptly he stood. "Excuse me, I'm not very hungry. See y'all later."

Wheeling, he made a beeline for the door. He was almost through it when he heard the scrape of chair legs and Dani's voice: "Me, either. I'm sorry...."

She was coming after him and she was loaded for

bear. Well, dammit, this time she was about to go too far!

HE WAS WAITING FOR HER in the open area between the barn and the house, and she could tell by his expression that he was good and mad. If he thought a good defense was a good offense in this case, she'd disillusion him in a hurry.

He'd betrayed her. There was no defense for that.

She walked right up to him and glared into his face. "Was your family *too* disappointed?"

"About what?"

"About your failure to soften me up enough to accept the first insulting offer that came along?"

"Soften you—! Are you kidding?" Lifting his hat, he rammed stiff fingers through his hair. "Just what are you accusing me of, Dani? Spit it out."

"Glad to." She jabbed a stiff forefinger into his chest. "Let's start with spying. I must admit, I wondered why a top hand like you would come to work here, and now I know. It was to keep an eye on us for your family, so that when the time was right they could swoop in and—and practically *steal* this place!"

"Spying!" He sputtered in outrage. "How could I be a spy when you knew who I was?"

"I certainly did not!"

"You didn't know from the day you arrived in town that I'm Jack Burke? Get a grip, girl."

"I knew you were Jack Burke, but I didn't know the

Burkes owned the XOX until today. You deliberately
kept me in the dark!"

"If you're in the dark," he drawled, "I'm not the
one who turned out the lights. Are you trying to tell
me you're really so dumb that you didn't know who
owned the XOX until you got an offer to buy the Bar
K?"

"I didn't even know then." She glared at him, de-
clining to defend herself against the "dumb" charge,
under the circumstances. "I didn't know until Dobe
told me, as a matter of fact."

Jack sucked in a deep, surprised breath. "I'd say
that doesn't make you any smarter than the law al-
lows," he announced.

"Are you denying you spied on us?"

"I sure as hell am."

"Then why did you let me maneuver you—"
damn, she was being rash "—*talk* you into working
here?"

"You got it right the first time. The word is defi-
nitely *maneuver*. And I came to work here because..."
He shook his head in evident disgust. "I owed your
father, that's why."

"Owed my father?" Her antenna shot up. "Owed
him what?"

"Not money!" He looked outraged, as if he'd read
her mind and didn't like the story. "I owed him a *favor*. He...did something for my grandpa, and I've
been trying to repay him ever since. But he died be-

fore—ah, what the hell." He turned his back on her. "Why am I trying to convince you, anyway?"

The sight of his broad back sent a fresh burst of exasperation through her. "Don't you walk away from me, Jack Burke! I'm not through talking to you yet!"

"Yeah, actually you are."

"I'm still the boss around here!" A note of panic infused her brave words and she took off after him.

"You're not *my* boss."

"I certainly am! Stop and—"

"No, Dani!" But he did stop on the bunkhouse steps and whirl to tower menacingly over her. "You're not my boss anymore because—" his eyes narrowed and his jaw hardened "—I *quit!*"

With those words, he disappeared inside the bunkhouse, leaving Dani in a state of shock.

JACK PACKED to leave the Bar K in a white-hot fury. Throw accusations at him, would she! He didn't take that kind of talk from anybody—well, with the possible exception of Grandpa, who'd pretty much accused him of the same thing: disloyalty.

Now that he stopped to consider, where *did* his loyalties lie?

He was a Burke and blood really was thicker than water, but he also felt such a pull toward Dani that it was almost irresistible. She intrigued him, she challenged him, she annoyed the hell out of him...and he kept coming back for more.

But not this time, he vowed. She'd gone too far. He

was going to write "paid in full" on that debt he owed her father and just get on with his life.

Sure he was...and he would thrust from his memory forever the lost, scared expression on her face when he said those final words: *I quit.*

DANI WAS STILL STANDING in front of the bunkhouse when Dobe and the boys approached with overt caution. At least she'd made up her mind.

If Jack wanted to leave, let him. She had enough men to carry on without him now.

Dobe halted several paces away, the others forming a half circle behind him. Their expressions were leery, their manner furtive.

Dobe cleared his throat. "Heard you and Jack caterwauling all the way back t' the house," he grumbled.

"I'm sorry if we disturbed your meal," she said stiffly.

"Didn't disturb *my* meal," he corrected her, "but you sure did make me curious."

It was on the tip of her tongue to point out that it really wasn't any of his business, but then another approach occurred to her. "Dobe, do you know anything about some...some debt Jack owed my father?"

His expression didn't change. "Yep," he said, and the three cowboys behind him nodded agreement. Apparently the whole world knew, with one notable exception.

"So what was it?" she prompted impatiently.

"I know," Dylan said, stepping forward. "Let me tell." He puffed up his chest importantly. "Awhile back, Jack's grandpa rolled his pickup—old man drives like a bat out of hell. Your pa pulled him outa the wreck just before it exploded." He looked around for validation, which was forthcoming with solemn nods of agreement.

Dani felt a sinking sensation in the pit of her stomach. "And so Jack..."

"That's right." Dobe took up the tale. "He was beholden to Wil Keene, the old son of a—the old reprobate. Jack done ever'thang he could think of for Wil, out of gratitude, don'cha know. But it was never enough and Wil lorded it over him somethin' awful. Then the old fool up and died so Jack took on you girls for his pay-back project."

Dani groaned. "I don't believe this."

"You better—" Dobe bristled "—because it's fact. That Jack Burke is true blue and you can take that to the bank. You're danged lucky to have him, that's fer sure."

Demoralized, she said in a strangled voice, "I'm afraid I *don't* have him, not anymore."

The cowboys hauled back in amazement. "What's that?" Dylan demanded.

"Jack." She gestured toward the bunkhouse. "He just quit." She added hastily, "But with the rest of you here, that won't be so bad. We'll get by if we all—"

"Forget it!" Joe Bob shook his head mightily. "If Jack's outa here, so am I."

"Me, too." Miguel and Dylan looked equally determined.

"But—but why? Haven't I been fair to you? Don't you like working here?"

"That's not the point," Dylan said sternly. "Jack talked us into comin' here—against my better judgment, I might add." He gave her a severe glance. "If he's leavin', I'm right behind him."

"And I'm right behind you," Miguel added. "You comin', Joe Bob?"

Joe Bob's lips tightened. "I hate to do it, Dani, because you've been fair and square with me. But Jack got me into this and if he ain't gonna be around to—"

The door to the bunkhouse swung open and Jack stood there, all tall and studly cowboy in his wrath. Dani stared at him as if she'd never seen him before.

And maybe she hadn't, not as Jack Burke, heir to a Texas Hill Country kingdom.

"What the hell's goin' on?" he snarled, hefting his duffel from one shoulder to the other.

"We're quittin' with you," Dylan announced. "Just wait'll we grab our gear and we can all split out of here."

"Hold on." Jack's jaws tightened. "Just because I'm leavin' doesn't mean the rest of you have to pull up stakes."

"Yeah," Joe Bob said, "it sure does."

Jack looked at Dani. "Is this the way you want it?"

"No!" She clenched her hands into impotent fists. "None of this is the way I want it, starting with—" She broke off, gritting her teeth. "Starting with you, Jack. I..." God, it was so hard to swallow her pride, but she had to do it, not only because she needed him so badly but because she'd desperately misjudged the situation. "I don't want *you* to go, either. But whether you go or stay, I...I owe you an apology."

Jack stared into her eyes, waiting; Joe Bob wasn't quite so patient.

"What for?" he asked. "What'd you do to him, Dani?"

"I didn't *do* anything," she snapped, "but I thought...I thought he'd done something... dishonorable." It was incredibly difficult to force the words out but she plowed on. "Now I realize I was just scared...and looking for explanations." She raised her face and met Jack's steady gaze. "I'm sorry," she whispered. "Will you forgive me for doubting you?"

For a very long moment, he stood perfectly still. Then he said, "Yeah, I will."

He hadn't agreed to stay, but even so, her heart soared. "I also release you from any further obligation you might feel toward my f-father. You've already repaid the Keenes a dozen times over." *But please don't walk away now*, her heart added in a silent cry.

He nodded curtly; his expression did not soften. "I appreciate that."

"Then..." There was nothing left to say, not really. She chewed on her lip, telling herself that if she had to beg to keep him—

"Is that all, then?" He said it coolly.

"Yes." *Speak up*, she importuned herself. *Grovel if you have to.*

"Because I've got to go put this stuff away again if you're done with me, boss lady." He turned back into the bunkhouse.

And at last she realized that he was going to stay and he hadn't made her beg...although he could have. At that moment, she wanted to throw her arms around his neck and cling to that broad chest and—

"In that case, we'll stay, too," Dylan announced happily.

"Hell," Dobe muttered, "this is much ado about hardly nothin'."

And they all trooped into the bunkhouse, while Dani stood there weak with relief, wondering if she'd really almost heard Shakespeare.

"OKAY, GRANDPA," Jack said the next day, "I cleared everything up with the Keenes, about you tryin' to buy their ranch out from under them. Don't you *ever* go behind my back like that again. If you decide to throw a monkey wrench into the gears in the future, at least have the gumption to tell me first."

"Okay," Austin said, "consider yourself tolt."

Jack frowned. "Tolt—I mean told what?"

"I'm about to fling that monkey wrench smack dab into your gears, boy."

"Now what?" As if he hadn't had enough hassles already this week.

"Muriel's done up and quit."

"Muriel's...?" Jack gawked. Of all the things he'd figured could go wrong at this particular moment, the housekeeper hadn't occurred to him at all.

"Friday's her last day. That's tomorrow."

"I know when Friday is," Jack said, irritated. "What's this got to do with me?"

"Plenty!" The old man leaped from his chair with the agility of a teenager. "Since you went over to the enemy, I've been doin' your work instead of carin' for Petey. But when Muriel goes, I gotta come back inside the house, don'cha see?"

"Hire someone else, then," Jack suggested, but he knew the flaw in that response before Austin even answered.

"I will," Grandpa snapped, "but findin' someone won't be easy and you doggone well know it. Then gettin' Petey used to her will be even harder. You remember how long it was before he took to Muriel? And even then, he'd druther be with his own kin that some strange *woman*."

"Okay, Grandpa, where's this goin'?"

"Right here—you gotta come back home and help out," Austin said flatly. "It's your bounden duty as a Burke. Petey needs you and the XOX needs you." His mouth turned down at one corner. "So what's it gonna be, boy, your own flesh and blood or a pack of strangers?"

JACK HAD TO FIND DANI and he had to find her fast, but she was in none of the usual places. Not in the barn, not in the house...

Grandma Tilly paused with her polishing rag held high, surrounded by the lemony smell of furniture wax. "I think she mentioned something about checking out the creek," she said uncertainly. "I know she sent a couple of the men to that far pasture to shore up some fences, and the other is cleaning up that trail up the hill to Lookout Point. That's all I know."

"Thanks, Granny."

She dimpled prettily. "Thank *you*, Jack. By the way, we're all real glad you decided to stay with us a bit longer."

"Glad to hear it," he said without enthusiasm. Until he spoke to Dani, he didn't want to let anybody else know about this new problem.

DOBE HAD TOLD DANI the small waterway meandering through the Bar K was called Handbasket Creek. Whatever it was called, it needed attention at this U-shaped bend, and she was prepared to give it.

Tethering Sundance, she set about dragging broken limbs and pieces of wood and other debris out of the shallow water and onto the gentle banks. Water, cold and clear in the sunlight, pooled deep behind nature's dam, but she soon had it flowing freely again.

The day couldn't have been more beautiful. The temperature had to be in the mid-seventies; grass and greenery seemed to have turned lush and lovely overnight. It was still much cooler back home in Montana, where this kind of green wouldn't appear for some time yet.

Struggling with her boots, Dani pulled each off in turn and set them side by side beneath a cottonwood. Then she scooted over to the edge of the embankment and dipped her feet in the water below.

Gasping at the chill, she yanked her feet out for a moment, then slowly lowered them again. This time she was prepared for the shock and withstood it bravely, although she closed her eyes against the icy jolt.

She'd got lucky the other day.

If Jack had pulled up stakes, the rest of them would have, too, leaving the Keene sisters little choice but to sell out and move on. But move on to where and to what?

Although they hadn't been here for very long, Dani had already fallen in love with the beautiful Texas Hill Country, and her own little piece of it in particular. There was nowhere else on earth she'd rather be, nothing else she'd rather be doing.

And Jack had made it possible in the face of his own family's ambition. She owed him for that. She really, really did.

Her ears pricked unexpectedly; was that the sound of a horse approaching slowly through the trees?

Eyes wide, she peered around, finally spotting Jack's bright sorrel picking his way carefully through the underbrush.

Jack was on the horse's back, naturally enough. Straightening, she gave him an offhand wave and tried to compose herself. She hadn't had a moment alone with him since she'd accused him of being her enemy, and she didn't quite know how to act.

The horse walked into the clearing and stopped. Jack sat, hands crossed over the horn, and looked down at her, his expression enigmatic. Then, without a word, he swung out of the saddle, tossing the reins down to ground-hitch the animal.

Still silent, he walked up to her and stood over her, an imposing figure so tall and strong. Still she felt no intimidation, but a little thrill of anticipation instead.

"Yes?" Her voice was a husky whisper. "Were you looking for me?"

He nodded. "There's something I have to tell you."

"Oh?" She licked her lips, her mind flying in a dozen different directions. "What is it, Jack?"

"Just this." He bent his knees and squatted beside her, so their gazes were more nearly level. "I'm afraid I've got some bad news."

Her stomach clenched. "Oh, God, what is it now?"

"Remember when I said I'd stay?"

"Of course I remember." No, no, this couldn't be happening again!

"I'm afraid everything's changed. I hate to do this

to you, Dani, but..." He sucked in a deep breath. "I quit."

AT FIRST HE THOUGHT she was going to flat pass out, and then he thought she might punch him in the nose. Of the two, he'd take the punch any day.

She flew to her feet as if shot from a gun. "You *what?*"

"I quit, but it's not my idea," he added, hastily rising. "See, our housekeeper's leaving tomorrow—"

"Your housekeeper?" She blinked as if he were speaking a foreign language. "What's that got to do with anything, unless you're the only one at the XOX who knows how to sweep the floors?"

"Well," he said, "sort of."

"Jack Burke, if you do this to me I—I'll kill you!"

She banged both fists on his chest, and he could feel her frustration. He caught her slender wrists and held them gently. "Dani," he said gruffly, "I'm sorry. I don't want to do this but—"

"Then don't!"

"No, wait, let me explain. It's Petey."

"Petey?" That got through to her and she gasped. "Is anything wrong with him?"

"Not yet, but here's the deal. Petey's not good with strangers. Muriel was already there when his folks died three years ago so he's used to her. But when she leaves it's gonna be a bitch to find someone he'll take to. In the meantime, Grandpa will have to take care of the kid. While he's doing that, somebody's got to tend the ranch."

"Your f-father?"

"Is traveling most of the summer. He's the point man for the exotic animals we raise. He has to represent the XOX, buying and selling." Jack shrugged, feeling helpless. "Somebody in the family's got to be in charge at the ranch."

"Petey's an orphan." It sounded so sad when she said it, as if she knew how that felt.

He nodded. "His father was my younger brother, Jim. Petey lost both parents at the same time and that's when he came to live with us—me and my pa and grandpa. We're all he's got, really."

"Then of course, you have to go back to the XOX."

She'd become so deathly calm that it scared him. Like she'd given up or something...

"I don't want to," he said desperately. "I said I'd stay and I intended to, but Petey..."

"Yes, Petey." She gave Jack a quick, shaky smile and he thought he saw tears trembling on her lashes. "Poor little boy in a house full of nothing but men! He'll grow up to be a woman hater."

"Nah, nothin' like that." But it made him uncomfortable to hear her say it. Petey sure wasn't going to get a good impression of the fairer sex from the three elder Burkes, that was for sure. "But I gotta admit, it'd do him good to be around women who were...you know, kinda motherly."

She nodded, in control again. "Or *grand*motherly,

like my granny." She sighed. "I like kids," she said softly, "and so do Toni and Niki. It's a shame...." Her voice trailed off even as her beautiful eyes widened.

It was a shame, he had to agree with that, but he had no idea why excitement suddenly transformed her expression.

He only knew he liked it.

She rose on tiptoes, grabbing his shirt with both hands. "Bring Petey to the Bar K," she exclaimed. "All of us love children and there would always be someone available to look out for him. Plus you'd be nearby and could spend all the time with him you like."

His heart leaped with relief, and yet he felt forced to say, "That's too big an imposition. The guests will be arriving soon and you'll all be too busy to look out for a kid."

"No, we won't. We'd be glad to do it."

He kept shaking his head. "You don't know all the stuff he can find to get into. He'll be a nuisance. He'll make messes. He'll—"

Jack could have thought of several more negatives if she hadn't risen on her tiptoes, uttered a short "Shut up!" and pressed her lips to his. In the flash of an eye, all his objections just plain disintegrated.

This was becoming familiar, he realized as her lips parted beneath his. The feel of her firm breasts pressed against his chest excited him further, as did the small hands that roamed over his arms and shoulders.

He heard some new, strange sound from her, a soft...*moan*, almost. Then she was pressing her hips against his and somehow it was almost as if she were becoming a part of him. His hands grasped her waist and slid up, until he was touching the soft sweet mound of her breast. A thrill shot through him, followed by a jolt of desire that nearly knocked him off his feet.

Her tender mouth drove him on, unleashing a melting combination of desire and profound tenderness. He wanted her so badly it hurt—literally and figuratively.

But here on a creek bank in the middle of an April day wasn't going to be the place he had her, for suddenly she braced her hands on his biceps and shoved herself out of his embrace. He had just a glimpse of her rosy-cheeked and confused face before she turned and stumbled a few steps away from him.

He watched her gasp for air, as he was gasping for air. When she turned, she had it together again.

"I'm sorry," she said, not as lightly as she perhaps had wanted. "That was my doing and—"

"Hey, it's not a problem." He felt the giddy grin curling at his lips and fought it back.

"You wouldn't stop talking."

"I'll remember that, since it works so well."

"Don't make fun of me," she ordered, but with a sheepish smile. "If it will make you happy, I'll ask for a vote of my sisters and grandmother on whether

Petey comes or not. If everyone is for it, will your father and grandfather allow it?"

He thought about that. "Yeah," he said, "I'm pretty sure I could talk them into it. Besides, it'd be good for the kid or I miss my guess."

"Good," she said, calm again although she still looked as if she'd just been kissed. "Let's ride back and lay the proposition on the table."

Man, he thought, following Dani and Sundance through the fields and pastures, a proposition was on his mind, but it didn't have a damn thing to do with Petey.

7

IT TOOK PETEY about ten minutes to conquer the Keene women and their grandma. With amused astonishment, Jack watched the kid take over the entire Bar K, guests and cowboys alike, by the end of the first day.

"Are all women that nuts about kids?" he asked Dani on the second day.

She edged away from him; she'd been doing that a lot since their encounter on the banks of Handbasket Creek. "Most of us," she admitted. "But you wait, we'll have *our* influence over him, too. This isn't as one-sided as it may appear."

"Few things are," he agreed, thinking of how she'd felt in his arms all hot and bothered—which hadn't been at all one-sided. He pulled his mind back to the subject at hand although it took considerable effort. "Don't drop your guard, though. Petey can be a pretty shifty character when he takes a notion."

"Come on, Jack!" She gave him an incredulous look. "How can you call a four-year-old shifty?"

"He's smart for his age?" He shrugged. "I'm not puttin' the kid down, I'm just warning you to stay alert."

"Not to worry," she said airily. "If four adult women and one adult man can't keep a rein on one adorable little kid, there's something wrong with the lot of us."

Jack knew when to let it drop so he changed the subject. "What have you decided about picking up a few more head of horses? If you don't, we'll have trouble mounting the rest of the folks who'll start pouring in here next week."

She made a wry face. "I think 'pouring in' may be laying it on a trifle thick. But you're right—we do need more stock. It's just that..." She chewed on her lower lip.

He figured he knew where she was headed. "Cash flow problems?"

She lifted her chin a notch. "Nothing I can't handle, but I may not be able to get as many horses as I'd like. The prices I've seen in the paper have been awfully high."

"Yeah, well..." *Shut up, Jack,* he told himself. *Don't get any more involved than you already are.* "I might..." *And then again, I might not. Pa and Grandpa are already madder than hell at me, so why do I want to make matters any worse?*

Travis and Austin had been particularly livid about his plan to bring Petey over here for the summer. They'd only given in when he'd pointed out that it would be a nice vacation for the boy with his uncle and four women at his beck and call. Petey could go home any time they wanted, for as long as they wanted.

They'd given in, although none too gracefully. If Jack hit them up so soon about selling horses to the Bar K, below market value...

Dani was looking at him with a puzzled expression. Lord, she was good-looking: so feminine and womanly, but at the same time so strong and determined. He admired her gumption more every day, not to mention her—

"You might what?" she finally demanded. "Do you know of any good deals out there? Because I sure could use one about now."

"Yeah, I think I might," he said over all those warning bells going off in his head. "Let me check it out and I'll get back to you."

She smiled. "Thanks, Jack. I can't tell you how much I appreciate this."

"I haven't done anything yet," he said, dismissing her appreciation because he wanted it so badly. "Now, about today's chores..."

"PETEY, COME BACK HERE!"

Grandma Tilly rushed after the fleeing youngster, her apron flapping in the breeze. She was laughing almost as hard as he was while pursuing him from stump to tree, from outbuilding to outbuilding. Catching up with him at last, she scooped him into her arms and pressed a kiss on his sweaty head.

Watching from the barn, Dani felt a twinge of

something very like longing. Jack had been right; Petey was a real handful, but he was also a charmer.

Just like his uncle.

Sighing, she turned abruptly and stopped short. Jack himself stood in the shadowy interior of the barn, apparently having entered from the back while she lingered at the front. She could barely make him out in the strong contrast of inside gloom to outside sunshine but she knew instantly who stood there so quietly.

"Is...everything all right?" she murmured. "You found the cattle okay and...and everything?"

"Yeah, no problems." He hauled off his leather gloves and slapped them against his thigh. "Everything on track here?"

She nodded, painfully aware of how dry her mouth was, how shallow her heartbeat. "Granny and Toni are going to take Petey to town with them this afternoon, if that's all right with you."

"It's fine with me."

"I thought it would be."

"What will you be doing?"

"I'll be finishing up cleaning the cabins. They're all done except for one—the John Wesley Hardin Cabin." She wrinkled her nose. "Jesse James and Billy the Kid I can understand, but John Wesley Hardin?"

Jack took a few steps toward her until he was close enough that she could see the curve of his lips despite the dimness. "Old John Wesley was a local boy," he said. "Pretty much stuck to Texas, but he was a very bad man indeed. Maybe you should read up on him in case any of your dudes ask."

"You're right." Increasingly nervous, she licked her lips. "What are the men doing this afternoon?"

"Still getting after those fences. I've got a couple of errands to run, and that'll be enough to keep them busy until I get back. That's if you don't have something else you want me to do."

"No, of course not. You know better than I do what needs to be done."

"I'll see you later, then."

He walked past her and into the sunlight. For a moment he stood framed by the huge opening, highlighted against brilliant sunlight. And suddenly Dani realized she was staring at his back with the same kind of longing with which she'd watched his nephew frolic across the yard.

She turned away abruptly. This was awful, the worst thing that could possibly have happened to her.

She was falling for a Texas cowboy. *Quick, call the men in the white coats!*

JACK DROVE STRAIGHT to the XOX. To his surprise, he found both his father and grandfather standing in the yard in front of the big house, deep in conversation— or maybe that was deep in disagreement. When he walked up, they didn't look to be in any too good a mood.

"Come to your senses yet?" Austin snapped before his grandson could get out a word.

"Maybe, maybe not." Jack grinned, thinking that at this point he didn't know where his senses even were, so how could he come to them? "I'm glad you're both here. I'm gonna sell six or eight head of horses to the Keenes and I wanted to tell you before I did it."

"You're *what?*" Travis barked. "Just like that, you're givin' away our horses?"

"That's not what I said. You decide what they're worth and that's what you'll get."

"Who from?" Austin demanded in his crotchety tone. "Who's payin', you or them wimmin?"

"They are." *Mostly*, Jack added silently. "Look, we've got more old tame saddle horses around here than we can feed. I won't short the XOX. You can count on it."

The two older men drilled him with grim disapproval. Jack forced himself to stand still before their daunting scrutiny, refusing to defend himself.

Travis said abruptly, "It might be cheaper to marry the girl."

"Marry...!" Jack's mouth dropped open. "Who said anything about *marriage?*"

"Me," Travis said. "Hell, I've been married twice and Pa's been hog-tied three times so I guess I oughta know the symptoms."

"This time you're wrong," Jack said heatedly. "I'm

thirty-goddamned-years-old and no woman's put a brand on me yet."

"Not too late, though." Austin glared at his grandson through narrow eyes. "How's she gettin' on with Petey?"

Jack blinked at the change of subject. "Fine. What's that got to do with anything?"

"Plenty. Likin' a man's dependents—or pretending to—is a shortcut to his heart. Why d'you think I married that Wanda woman? She was absolutely crazy about my grandsons, is why. Till she got her brand on me and then she not only didn't like you and Jim, she didn't even much like *me* no more."

"That was you. Dani's not pretending a damned thing." Jeez, he shouldn't have said her name.

Austin and Travis exchanged shifty glances and the younger man said, "I told you it was the one named Dani."

"It's *not* the one named Dani," Jack objected hotly. "She just happens to be the one who handles the business end of things at the—" He stopped short. "Why the hell am I arguing with you two? You're just trying to get my goat. I'll give you an accounting of the horses I take. After you give me a bill, I'll see it gets to the right place." He spun away.

"Meanin' you'll pay the difference," Austin called after Jack.

"What if I do? You know I—"

Simultaneously the two finished with him, their voices singsong: "Owe Wil Keene."

Jack threw open the door to his pickup, but before he could flee the scene, his grandpa got in the last word: "And we're gettin' awful danged tired of hearing about that!"

DANI FOUND the guest cabins charming if rustic.

Each was basically the same: one large room with either one queen-size bed or twin beds, a sofa and coffee table, a couple of bureaus and a closet for clothes, plus a small bathroom with a shower in the tub. Beds were covered with identical, well-worn, woven spreads with a chenille reproduction of the Bar K brand: a curving quarter circle with a capital *K* on top of it.

The furniture was, to put it mildly, eclectic. Some pieces looked like flea-market finds, while others might be genuine antiques. Hardwood floors, scarred but mellow, added to the atmosphere. As a bow to modern life, every cabin was air-conditioned—praise the Lord, Dani thought, throwing open the windows and doors of the John Wesley Hardin Cabin to let in light and air. From what she'd heard of Texas summers, she wouldn't want to face one without air-conditioning.

Here it was, only April, and already the air was heavy with humidity and temperatures edging up every day. As a native of Montana, she was less than sure how she'd take to the weather here.

But everything else she loved. If they could only

get this place up and running, then hang on long enough to start turning a profit...

She paused, arms full of linens and head cocked, trying to catch the sound that had arrested her attention. It almost sounded like...

Horses! A whole herd of horses! Tossing the sheets and pillowcases onto the couch, she hurried out on the small covered porch. Shading her eyes from the brightness, she peered toward the narrow dirt road that led to the main house.

In the distance rose a small plume of dust, moving nearer and nearer until she could see—

Horses, driven by a lone rider. Jack, of course, bringing the animals they needed to fill out their herd. Jack to the rescue yet again.

That terrible sharp longing swept over her, almost expected by now. He'd really been so awfully good to them—maybe too good. She'd released him from any obligation he might still feel toward her father, but was he doing all this because he still felt beholden?

From the road, he saw her and raised his hat in a salute, pointing it toward the pasture and corral near the barn. She nodded and set off behind the house, aiming to beat him there so she could open the gate.

Breathlessly she watched the horses stream past, eight of them, all fat and sleek and tailor-made for her purposes. A cloud touched her horizon. Could she afford such good animals?

Jack swung off a bay wearing the XOX brand.

"What do you think?" he challenged. "Is this what you had in mind?"

"They're perfect. Only..." Dani bounced on her toes with excitement. "Are you sure I can afford them? I mean, they look great, if they're gentle enough for beginners." A sudden thought occurred to her and she settled back on her heels. "But all these horses wear the XOX brand. I don't want charity, Jack."

"What charity?" He turned to loosen the saddle girth. "The XOX is horse poor, as Grandpa would say. Don't worry, you'll get a bill, just like anyone else."

"I'd better. I just hope it's not *too* high." Now the worries really set in. "I'm not sure we can afford eight, actually."

"Fat old horses like this are a dime a dozen." He led his horse to the corral, opened the gate and slipped off the bridle, releasing the animal with a pat on the rump. "Trust me, you'll be surprised at how cheap horses can be in Texas."

"In that case..." She stepped up to him and threw her arms around him to give him a well-deserved hug.

Just a hug, nothing else. At least not on her part.

"Thank you so much," she murmured, her lips brushing his shirt while her fingers dug into his waist. "If I thought you were subsidizing us—"

"Who, me? I haven't laid out a penny." His arms closed around her, strong and possessive.

"You better not, either." She could barely find the breath to say it.

For a moment they stood there in each other's arms. Then Dani pushed back with an anxious laugh.

"You probably should check out the horses a little better," he said quickly. "If there's any you don't like—"

"Good grief, Jack." She gave him a quizzical look. "Don't you think I know by now that any horse you say is okay is okay?"

"Yeah, well, I just thought..."

"Okay, if you say so, but I really don't have time now. I've still got the John Wesley Hardin Cabin to take care of. Everything's all scrubbed down, but I have to make the bed and get everything back in its place. Maybe after that—"

"How about I give you a hand?" he inquired, his voice gruff. "Then you'll be finished quicker and we can ride out and let you really look them over."

Her scalp prickled, whether with anticipation or alarm, she couldn't be sure. "Oh, I don't think you want to do that."

"Hell," he said, "I know how to make a bed."

He probably did. "Sure," she agreed impulsively. "Why not? I'll just finish that much faster."

Or *get* finished.

HER LOOK OF JOY AND RELIEF as she'd watched the horses stream past had nearly undone him. If Pa and

Grandpa charged him double what the animals were worth, he'd pay it without a whimper.

Standing across the bed from him, shaking out the fitted bottom sheet and then waving it in the air to let it waft down on the mattress, she still looked happy and excited and...absolutely, totally, completely desirable.

"Well?" she demanded, holding her edge of the sheet. "I thought you were here to help me!"

"Yeah, sorry." He grabbed for the sheet, but not before admitting, at least to himself, that he wasn't here to help her at all.

He was here to look at her, to catch any smile that might cross her face, to argue with her and maybe...just maybe...

"Jack! You've got to pull the elastic around the corner and tuck it under. Are you sure you ever made a bed before?"

She was laughing at him, and rightly so. He was just standing there holding the edge of the sheet as if he'd never seen one before.

He hadn't, not across a bed from Dani Keene.

"I may not be good at makin' beds," he said, "but I sure do know what they're for." And with a little tug, he brought her tumbling forward across the quilted mattress and unsecured sheet.

"Oh!" She struggled to sit up, succeeding only in tangling herself up the sheet. "Jack Burke, what do you think you're do—"

She ended on a little shriek because she saw what

he thought he was doing: joining her. On his knees on the bed, he lifted her and wrapped his arms around her.

"Just look at me the way you looked at that herd of horses and I'll be happy," he muttered, his voice rough. "Dani, you're drivin' me crazy!"

"I'm a little c-crazy myself," she gasped, leaning into him. "Otherwise I wouldn't be here like this...with you...doing this."

"You're not doing anything...yet." He pressed his lips to her temple, smoothing back her hair with hands that shook. "Would you rather be here with someone else, then?"

She sighed and her breath warmed his throat. "No, oh Lord no. I don't have time for...don't have room for *any* man in my life."

She sure wasn't acting as if she meant that. He kissed his way down her cheek to her throat, and she turned her head to allow him free access to the satin skin. Her breathing had become heavy and uneven, and the pulse at the base of her neck pounded beneath his probing tongue.

He cupped the generous curves of her breasts with his hands and still she leaned closer instead of away. What she murmured astounded him: "Oh, Jack, that feels so *good*...."

"To me, too." He found her mouth at last and kissed her, drinking in the sweetness she offered so freely. Without artifice, she met the thrust of his tongue with her own.

Holding her, he fell to his side on the bed, taking her with him. Face to face and body to body, they kissed again and again as they explored each other with hands that shook with mounting passion. When he unbuttoned her blouse, she made no protest. When she unbuckled his belt, he didn't protest, either—but he thought he might explode when she thrust a hand down the front of his jeans.

By then, he'd found the waist of *her* jeans and with artful tugging relieved her of them. He reached for her thigh and her hand shot out to catch his wrist. For an eternity, he stared into vulnerable brown eyes, and then she caught her breath and said a disbelieving, "Oh, what the hell!" and guided his hand to the very place it wanted to be.

Wrestling around in the tangled sheets, twisting and contorting, they managed to rip the rest of their clothing away. It would have taken about half the time it did if they hadn't each been so intent on touching and being touched, but at last it was accomplished. They lay panting and naked on the messy bed, side by side and heart to heart.

"I've been waitin' for this ever since the first day I saw you, leading old Sundance around the Y'all Come Café," Jack muttered, stroking down her belly. "I swear, Dani, I've never wanted anything as bad in my life as I want you." He slid his hand between her thighs and she opened them just a fraction wider to accommodate him. "Not even Santa Claus ever gave me anything I wanted this much."

"Then get ready for a real merry Christmas," she said, one small hand closing over his hardness. "I always say, if you're gonna do a thing, at least do it ri—" She caught her breath on a husky groan, for he'd found what he sought and her body bucked against his hand.

Her reaction devastated him. He wanted to crawl all over her, sink into the depths of her, but it wasn't quite time yet. Moving his hand rhythmically, he bent over her breast and fumbled a pebbled nipple into his mouth, then sucked it deep while his tongue teased and tickled. By the time he lifted his head, she was almost sobbing with reaction.

"You okay?" He hefted the weight of her breast in the palm of his hand.

"Yes." It was a groan and she shifted restlessly. "It's just that...you're driving *me* crazy!"

"I was kinda hopin'." He lifted her breast to his lips with one hand, while with the other he explored lower. She gasped and opened wider.

He could go on like this forever—but only in theory; if he did, he'd explode into a zillion pieces before the game was played out. Rising, he rolled over her, fumbled for his jeans and the condom he'd deliberately shoved into his pocket before he'd left home with the horses. Then, braced on stiff arms, he moved between her thighs at last.

She touched his penis, directed it toward her trembling heat. The tip touched the entrance to her body and she let out a soft moan. She was tight, but he slipped inside with care, then held himself still for an instant, unable to believe that they had come this far this quickly.

And then he didn't think at all, just moved inside her, easy and careful at first, but then with ever more powerful thrusts. She rose to meet him, urging him on, harder and deeper until he felt his control crumbling.

She moaned softly and he kept up his rhythm, aware of her body's unbridled response. It nearly equaled his, for he was flying up there someplace around the ceiling.

She convulsed suddenly, the cords in her neck standing out and her eyes closing while her lips formed an astonished "Oh!" That did it. Jack's body tensed and he knew the time had come. Aware of every sensation, he felt his body working toward a climax shattering in its intensity.

With a groan he surrendered to it, neck arching back and lips parting over the sound: *Yesss!* No longer able to support his own weight, he dropped heavily to lie upon her still-quivering body.

"I'm sorry...." Gasping, he tried to roll aside, fearing he'd crush her.

Her arms tightened around him and she held him there, her velvety voice murmuring in his ear, "It's all right...don't move, just feel...."

And that's what he did, for a very long time.

EVENTUALLY DANI EMERGED from her sensual fog. Staring past his shoulder at the plain white ceiling, she confronted the question that wouldn't go away: *What have I done?*

Never in her entire life had she been so carried away by passion. Passion growing between them from the very first day they met, although she'd warily avoided the truth just as long as she could.

Self-deception ended here, in this bed. Now that she knew the truth, she could guard against it. She could—

He rolled off her with a groan and she resisted the impulse to try to hold him there. He was right; she could barely breathe. But somehow that didn't seem nearly so important as hanging on to this moment as long as she possibly could.

"You okay?" He settled beside her, head propped on a hand. "I was afraid I'd squash you."

"I must not look as tough as I am." Suddenly aware of something besides fabulous sex, she realized that she was naked and so was he. They lay in a tangle of sheets in the John Wesley Hardin Cabin. It was too late to go all modest and self-conscious now, so she resisted the urge to pull a crumpled length of cotton over her nakedness.

"Actually, you do look pretty tough most of the time." He rubbed her lower lip lightly with his thumb. "Now I know it's all an act."

She gave a self-conscious little laugh. "Don't be so sure."

"I'm sure, all right." He dropped a kiss on the

smooth curve between her arm and her shoulder. "Have I told you lately how fabulous you are?"

Now she *was* embarrassed. Sitting up, she swung her legs over the side of the bed and looked around for her clothing, discarded in such haste. She tried to speak lightly but was aware of the underlying seriousness when she said, "Don't try to sweet-talk me."

"Why not?"

He kissed the dimples at the base of her spine and she jumped as if shot. "Stop that!" She batted at him behind her back without turning around.

He caught one of her hands and pressed a kiss on her vulnerable palm, then let out a gusty sigh. "This could be habit-forming," he said, his tone halfway between teasing and challenging. "I'd *like* it to be habit-forming."

"I'm glad you brought that up." Bending, she snatched her underwear off the floor. "This is not the real me, Jack."

"Then who is it? I want to meet her!"

"Don't laugh at me." She darted him an incensed glance, but his obvious delight brought a sheepish smile to her face.

"If I can't laugh, what should I do?" He smoothed his palms over the curves of her hips.

"Listen!" Jumping up, she kept her back to him while she pulled on her underthings and reached for her jeans and shirt. Fortified by clothing, she faced him. "I'm sure you're as aware as I am that what just happened was a huge mistake."

He frowned. "You're kidding."

"Certainly not. The truth is..." She finished buttoning her shirt and straightened, belatedly realizing how sexy it was to stand fully clothed above a naked man. She swallowed hard and tried again. "The truth is, I have no intention of getting serious about any man until I'm at least thirty."

"Who said anything about getting serious?" Frowning, he sat up. "*I* didn't say anything about getting serious. You intend to wait until you're thirty to get serious? Well, I'm not sure I *ever* intend to get serious. That doesn't mean I intend to stop living, though." A significant glance at the bed conveyed exactly what he meant by "living."

Dani uttered an exasperated sigh. She hadn't expected this response from him at all. They'd seemed so close, so in tune, but apparently she'd misread his feelings. She was obviously no more to him than an easy lay. That knowledge lent steel to her spine.

"Whatever," she snapped. "It was a dumb mistake that I don't intend to repeat."

"You're sure about that." He obviously didn't believe her.

"Absolutely."

He pulled on his jeans, covering a vast expanse of male flesh. Her determination hardened. "In fact," she added, "I'm going to forget this ever happened. I suggest you do the same."

"I don't think I can do that." His blazing hazel eyes

challenged her. "I don't think you can forget it so easily, either."

"I certainly can." She turned away. "Just watch me."

Dumb, really dumb. The last thing she wanted to do was issue a challenge.

8

DANI AND JACK WERE warily smoothing the bed-
spread into place in the John Wesley Hardin Cabin
when the sound of the Jeep entering the front yard
brought them both upright. They exchanged
glances—hers guilty, his wary.

She tightened her lips disapprovingly. What had
happened had happened and there was nothing she
could do about that now. She wouldn't think about it,
she wouldn't feel guilty about it, she wouldn't...hope
it would happen again. Especially not that!

"They're back." She stated the obvious.

"Shame." The corner of his broad mouth quirked
up and his hazel eyes sparkled impishly.

She didn't dignify that with an answer, just gave
the neat bed a final pat, picked up her bucket of cleaning supplies and walked out onto the porch. Jack followed. Crossing the yard toward the house, Petey
saw them and veered in their direction.

"Uncle Jack, I got a ice-cream cone!" he shouted. "I
got a toy!" He waved a brightly colored plastic action
figure in the air.

Toni and Grandma followed the boy, their expressions first bemused, then knowing as they took in the

sight of Jack and Dani standing side by side on the cabin porch.

Jack frowned at the women. "I don't want you spending money on Petey," he said. "If you'll tell me how much, I'll—"

"I declare," Granny said. "It was just a pittance. Don't worry about a thing." She added to Dani, "Did you manage to get any work done?" Her mischievous glance skipped to Jack.

"Certainly," Dani said stiffly. "The cabin's all ready." She brightened. "And something else happened, too."

Toni laughed. "I kinda thought so."

Dani felt her cheeks burn with embarrassment. "Very funny," she said, her tone cross. "I mean something good."

"So did I."

"Darn it, Toni—"

"What Dani's trying to tell you," Jack interjected smoothly, "is that I found a few horses for sale at a decent price and brought them on over. They're in the pasture."

Toni's eyes widened. "That's fantastic, Jack! Honestly, I don't know how you do it but you always come through for us."

"It's a gift," he said with false modesty, kidding around.

"But the horses aren't a gift," Dani said quickly, giving him a severe glance. "We'll pay a fair price for them."

Toni sighed. "Let's just hope we don't have any un-expected expenses getting up to speed for the tourist season. I swear, Dani, our bank account is just melt-ing away."

"Don't worry, we'll be fine," Dani said with a con-fidence laid on for the occasion, because she really wasn't sure about that at all. Their financial situation was a constant worry.

Jack looked down thoughtfully at Petey, sitting on the steps examining his new toy. "You know," he said in a musing tone, "it was a real surprise around here when we heard Wil's estate didn't include a big hunk of cash."

"How do you know it didn't?" Dani challenged.

"Hell, I expect we knew it before y'all did." His glance included the lot of them. "Remember, this is a small town."

Granny nodded. "And we know about those, girls. Jack, what made you think Wil *had* any money? When I knew him, he didn't have two nickels to rub to-gether."

"Because he inherited everything Miss Elsie had," he responded promptly. "He cleaned out her bank accounts after her death and she was rumored to have a big insurance policy, but nobody knew what he did with all that cash. Since it wasn't mentioned in the will, all we can figure is that maybe he lost it gam-bling or on bad investments."

"Or maybe," Dani said tartly, "there wasn't any money at all."

"Even so, Miss Elsie had a lot of jewelry," Jack said reasonably. "Most of it was old family stuff, but at least the stones had to be valuable. There was one emerald necklace she used to wear to parties that was pretty famous around here."

Dani shrugged. "A moot point, I'd say, since we haven't seen a single diamond lying around." She picked up the bucket of cleaning supplies she'd set outside the door earlier. "Look, I've got work to do. The rest of you can stand around and shoot the breeze, but you'll have to excuse me."

"Me, too." Jack stepped off the porch. "Petey, you be good, okay?"

"Okay." The little boy turned an angelic smile on his uncle.

Dani walked back to the house deeply depressed. The triplets had been poor all their lives and had struggled to hold the family together. If their father had blown a fortune and left them only a run-down dude ranch without the money to support it, she shouldn't be too surprised. It was just one more censure to lay at his door.

But it would be nice just once in her life not to have to worry about making ends meet....

AVOIDING JACK WASN'T EASY, but Dani managed to do it, at least when the others weren't around. Toni and Grandma apparently clued Niki in on what they *thought* was going on because all three of them were watching with eagle eyes and many conspiratorial glances.

Let them! Dani had no intention of dropping her guard with that long tall cowboy ever again. Hence there was nothing to see, now or ever.

There was plenty to feel, though, not the least of which was a yearning for a repeat performance of their encounter in the Wes Hardin Cabin. Sometimes she simply couldn't help thinking about they way they'd tumbled around on that bed like a couple of eager kids and...and—

She stood up abruptly from the lunch table, making a point of not looking at Jack, who sat between Dylan and Miguel, chowing down on Granny's enchiladas. "I'm going into town to pick up a few things," she announced, her tone much too cranky and impatient for the situation. "Anyone want anything?"

"Not me." Toni glanced at Grandma, who gave a who-knows widening of her eyes.

"Then I'll see you later." Dani stalked out of the room. Out of Jack's annoying presence, she felt an immediate lifting of her bad mood.

All she needed was a little time away from all this pressure. When she returned, she'd be her old self again.

HER PLAN MIGHT HAVE worked if she hadn't bumped into an old guy with wispy white hair and far-seeing blue eyes at the grocery store. She'd gone in to pick up a couple of novels to while away those dreaded hours of memory.

Literally.

Rounding a corner, she nearly knocked the old guy down. Grabbing his arm to help him regain his balance, she proceeded to apologize profusely.

"I'm so sorry! My goodness, I'm not in the habit of mowing down innocent bystanders. Are you all right? I *do* apologize."

The old guy righted himself and gave her a dubious glance. "You come around that corner like a bat outa hell," he accused. "What's so all-fired important—" He stopped short, his eyes widening.

Was he having some delayed reaction to almost being knocked down? "I was thinking about something else and not paying attention," she admitted, watching him closely. "Are you sure you're all right? Maybe you ought to sit down for a minute."

"Calm down, girl. I'm fine," he said impatiently. "Say, are you one of them Keene gals that took over the Bar K?"

She nodded. "I'm—"

"Don't tell me, let me guess. You're Dani."

Startled, she took a step back. "That's right. How did you know?"

"My grandson described you to a T."

"You're Jack's grandfather?" Her stomach heaved.

"The one and only."

"He talked to you about me?" Affronted, she forgot that she was in the wrong.

"Sure." He shrugged, as if they discussed her all the time—as if Jack reported to him! "You paid for them horses yet?"

"I haven't even got the bill yet," she said defensively.

"It's in his pocket. If you can't come up with the cash," the old man suggested with a grin she interpreted as evil, "you can always put it against what we're willin' to pay for the Bar K."

"I can—what?" She stared at him, aghast. "Mr. Burke, I can't believe what I'm hearing. Is this just another scheme to get the ranch away from us?"

"I didn't say that a'tall." He lifted his white Stetson in farewell. "Nice runnin' into you. Too bad you won't be around long enough fer me to get to know you."

"That's what *you* think—sir." She spoke with tight jaws. "I'm going to be around for a long, long time, and you can *just get used to it.*"

AUSTIN GRINNED MIGHTILY. "And then she told me she was gonna be here for a long time and I could *just get used to it,*" he reported to son and grandson. "I'll say one thing for her, that Dani Keene's got spunk and I purely love spunk."

Jack groaned. "I told you that. Why'd you have to go pick a fight with her?"

"Me? Me!" Austin looked greatly offended by the suggestion. "She picked the fight, I didn't. I just told her she could put what she owed on the horses against what we'd pay her for the ranch. I thought it was danged nice of me to point that out."

"Pa," Travis said, "you oughta be ashamed." But his wide grin belied his words.

"Oh, I am," Austin agreed. "Ashamed I let that little slip of a girl have the last word." He laughed and punched his grandson on the arm. "Cheer up, Jack. You said yourself you don't have a *thang* goin' with that girl so why so glum?"

"Because—well, you—don't think—" Jack sputtered to a halt. "Grandpa, sometimes I think you just like to cause trouble. She was already mad at me and now..." He shuddered at the thought. "I'm outa here."

"Where y'goin'?" Travis yelled after him. "I hope it's to get the money for those horses!"

Not hardly, Jack thought, driving back to the Bar K. He had a bill in his pocket, all right, but not one that Dani would ever see. First chance he got he'd make out a duplicate for about half of what the horses were worth and present it to her, then pay the other half himself. But he hadn't had time to do that yet and now something more important had come up.

Because if he didn't smooth over his grandpa's bad impression, the chances of ever getting her back into bed were slim and none, which just plain wasn't acceptable to a man for whom *once* truly was not enough.

DANI WAS IN THE TACK ROOM polishing saddles when Jack walked in. She'd propped open the hinged wooden panels covering unscreened openings that let in pleasant April breezes. She'd seen him coming and noted the grim expression on his face.

She gave him a cool glance and went back to her work, but that was only subterfuge. She knew what she had to do, but needed to wait until her pulse had returned to normal before doing it.

Jack skidded to a halt before her. "Look, about what Grandpa said—"

She looked up sharply. "Which part?"

Jack blinked. "How many parts are there? I mean, when he brought up buying the ranch."

"Oh, that." She skimmed her rag over the tin of saddle soap.

"Don't pay any attention to him," he urged. "That's just the way he is. He likes to put people on."

"Really? I got the very strong impression that he detested me before he ever met me."

"Nah, he likes you. He said you've got spunk."

"I've got spunk all right, but if that's how he treats people he likes—!" Tossing her stained rag on the saddle, she stood up. "Look, I want the bill for those horses." She held out her hand.

He took a skittish step back. "I'll bring it tomorrow."

"I want it today."

"But I don't have it today." He was beginning to look a trifle desperate.

She advanced. "Yes, you do. Your grandpa said you had it in your pocket."

"I say I don't." Apparently realizing escape was impossible, he squared his shoulders and faced her. "What are you gonna do, search me?"

"If I have to." She stopped just inches from touching him, so close she could feel the heat of his body. "What are you hiding, Jack?"

"Nothing," he blustered. "Not a damned thing."

So what *was* she going to do? He was too strong for her to wrestle him into submission. Wrestle... There was, after all, another kind of wrestling....

"All right," she said. "If you say you don't have it, I guess I have no choice but to accept that." But she didn't move away from him.

"That's more like it." His relief was obvious. "I...I'm sorry you had to meet Grandpa that way. He's not a bad old guy under normal circumstances."

"Really?" She'd thought he *was* a bad old guy, and the twinkling eyes hadn't fooled her for an instant. Reaching up, she touched Jack's chest lightly with her fingertips.

One of them gasped and recoiled slightly; she wasn't sure which. Maybe it was both.

Quickly he covered her hand with his to stop all movement, but he didn't push her away. "What are you up to?" he demanded, looking down into her up-turned face suspiciously. "Aren't you the one who claimed you were going to forget we ever—"

"Don't go there," she said quickly. "That's much too..." Intimate? Personal? Thrilling?

He lifted her hand and pressed it against his cheek, then slid his arm around her waist. "Yeah," he said gruffly, "it's much *too*, all right. Are we, uh, starting up again?"

"Absolutely not." But she couldn't resist pressing her hips against his hardness and sighing. "Jack, I'm weak," she confessed, thinking it was part of her plan to disarm him. "I never thought so before but..."

"But you had a hard time forgetting?" His brows flew up. "Dani, I won't forget if I live to be a hundred, and I don't want to forget. What happened to us in the John Wesley Hardin Cabin was—was..."

She held her breath, not sure what word she'd use there, either. Maybe spectacular...maybe lovely... maybe *insane!*

Giving up the semantic struggle, he leaned down and pressed his lips to hers. A too-familiar shock streaked through her, stealing away her breath. No longer was this a voyage of discovery, for now they knew what could happen—and wanted it.

He slipped one knee between her thighs to get closer still. She wrapped a leg around his, her groan lost in his mouth. Without taking his hands off her, he backed her against the brace holding the window open and it slammed down.

Immediately the room, filled with saddles and bridles and other horse accoutrements, darkened. In the increased intimacy, he fumbled for the buttons on her shirt, the buckle on her belt.

While she, she—! How could she stop him when every fiber of her being demanded to be joined with his? She'd never imagined she could want like this, to the point of utter distraction. All the details of their previous intimate encounter swamped her and she wanted that again, so desperately that she found herself tugging at his clothing as he was hers.

"Ah...yes."

His fingers coaxed dampness. Pleasure shot through her, so intense that her legs nearly buckled. This was insane, being wrapped around each other this way in the middle of the afternoon in a semi-public place where anyone could walk in at any minute, yet she couldn't dredge up the will to pull away.

She wanted what he was giving her and more, wanted to give back the same and more. His hands and mouth upon her body and hers upon his, leading inevitably and inexorably to that magic moment of joining....

She'd started something she might not be able to stop unless she acted immediately and without calculating what she'd be losing.

She thrust her hand into his jeans pocket, touched something that felt like paper and yanked it out. He said, "What the hell?" in a groggy voice and lifted his head to peer at her, his eyes hazy.

She stumbled back, fumbling to get her clothing into some semblance of order before unfolding the sheet of paper. Before he could stop her, her gaze flew to the bottom of the page, where the total was written in big black figures.

"My God!" She stared at him in shock. "Is this a joke?"

"Jeez." He looked anguished, but it might have been mostly physical. "Why'd you have to go and do that for?"

"Because you were lying to me. This is my bill. You were supposed to *give* it to me!" She hadn't imagined she was capable of going to such lengths to get it, though—or that the bill would be so high it would nearly wipe out their emergency fund to pay it.

"You don't understand." He looked desperate.

"What's to understand?" Her voice trembled, but so did her body—with disappointment. "This bill is about twice what I thought it would be. Not that I think the Burkes would inflate prices—hell, they don't have to. We're babes in the woods. I suppose this is what we get for playing with the big boys."

"It's not like that," he said, his tone pleading. "I was going to—I mean, the idea was to—"

"Give it up, Jack," she snapped. "Is this an honest price for those horses or not?"

"Yes, but—"

"Then there's nothing more to be said." Something felt as if it were breaking inside her and it might be her heart. "If we couldn't pay this bill, I suppose your plan was to put more pressure on us to sell."

"That's not it at all."

"There's no other possibility unless you intended to pay some or all of this bill yourself." She glared at him. "You damned well know I'd never stand for that."

"No," he agreed, "I don't suppose you would unless—"

"*Fire!*"

They looked at each other in confusion, so deep in their own little drama that it took a moment for the meaning of the word to sink in:

Fire!

EMERGING FROM the tack room at a run, Jack looked around quickly to discover the source of danger. Ahead he saw Grandma Tilly racing across the yard toward Toni, who stood outside a small outbuilding used for storage.

At least, that's what Jack thought it was used for. In the rush to get ready to open, he hadn't bothered to look inside and didn't think anyone else had, either. Small and shabby and out of the way, its priority was low.

That didn't mean they could just let it burn to the ground, which it seemed about to do as smoke poured from the far corner of the structure. Changing angles, Jack dashed toward the bunkhouse, the building nearest to the flames and the spot where he knew he'd find a hose already connected to a water spigot. Grabbing the nozzle, he turned on the faucet and pointed the stream of water toward the burning building.

"Hey, watch out!" Dani had managed to get between Jack and the fire, and the rush of water nearly knocked her down.

"Sorry!" he shouted, dragging the hose closer. "Toni, get back! Grandma, don't go in there!"

"Petey—!"

Petey! Jack's heart stopped beating.

"He's safe," Toni yelled. "He's over there next to the house!" She pointed.

Jack took an instant to snatch a look; the boy squatted a safe distance away, poking at the dirt between his cowboy boots with a stick and watching the goings-on with great interest.

Dani came alongside the boy, dragging the hose connected to the faucet beside the house. Water dripped from her hair, but she looked anything but bedraggled with her eyes blazing as brightly as the flames Jack should be fighting.

But he didn't have time to think about her or about what had just happened between them. His relationship with this woman was getting too damned complicated for a simple cowboy.

First he'd put out the fire in the building. Then he'd put out the fire in himself—he hoped to God.

DANI AND JACK STOOD side by side, staring at smoldering embers at the corner of the storage structure.

Jack pointed his hose at the spot and the final glowing cinders hissed, sizzled and went out.

"Well, hell," he said. "Do you want me to quit or are you going to fire me?"

"What?" She glanced at him in confusion. "You didn't have anything to do with this fire...did you?"

He gave her a glance that would curdle milk. "I'm not talking about the fire, I'm talking about the horses. You think I had some sinister motive for bringing them here, so surely you don't want me around any longer."

Did she? At this point, she couldn't be sure. But finally looking at him, she faced an undeniable fact: whether she wanted him here or not, she needed him.

Desperately.

So she said, "Don't be ridiculous. You know I can't get along without you."

He gave her a startled glance and turned quickly away. Was it guilt he felt? She certainly hoped so.

"You can take all the time you need to pay for the horses," he said at last. "No hurry."

"*I'm* in a hurry. Come into the house and I'll write you a check."

"Damn, you're stubborn." He sounded disgusted again.

"So I'm told." Turning, she marched back to the house, her own words ringing in her ears: *You didn't have anything to do with this—did you?*

He hadn't really answered her, she realized now. What if he did know something about the fire? What if he'd deliberately set out to keep her occupied while a confederate did that dirty deed?

No, it couldn't be true, and yet...why would anyone bother to torch that more or less useless building unless it was a warning?

Was someone out to sabotage them until they had no choice but to sell the ranch...and was Jack Burke involved?

9

NATURALLY, THE FIRE WAS topic number one at the dinner table. Even Petey seemed interested.

"I liked that fire," he declared. "It was pretty."

Granny handled that one. "Good gracious, no," she said firmly. "You must stay far away from fires, young man."

"But—"

"Listen to her," Jack said sternly. "Fires are dangerous and they can hurt nosy little boys."

Dani patted the pouting child on the shoulder. "Petey understands, don't you, honey?" She raised her gaze to the adults. "Let's get down to brass tacks. There was no great loss, thank heavens. We hadn't even had time to sort through the junk in that building. Since our first guests will be arriving tomorrow..."

She took a deep breath, thinking that things were moving so fast she could hardly keep them straight in her own mind. The fire *could* have been started by natural causes, after all. "I think what we should do now is just ignore the whole thing until we get our guest operation running smoothly," she concluded.

After a moment's silence, Jack said, "Do you really think that's a good idea?"

Niki, home for dinner on her day off, frowned. "Good idea or bad, we don't have much choice," she pointed out. "There's just so much time in a day."

Dylan leaned forward eagerly. "But there's something you folks don't know." He stuck out his fist. Uncurling his fingers one by one, he spilled several small charred pieces of wood onto the tabletop, then waited expectantly for their reaction.

Dani frowned. "Where'd you find the matchsticks, Dylan?"

"Right where the fire started," he responded. "Or maybe I should say, where the fire *was* started."

"Arson?" Jack's eyes narrowed.

"That's how I figure it. Maybe we should call the law."

Dani shook her head. How would it look to have policemen milling around when the guests arrived? "What good would that do?" she argued. "Nobody saw anybody lurking. Plus, having lawmen poking around would sure put a damper on our first week in business."

"But—"

"We don't *know* somebody started the fire," she interrupted. "Anything could have been in that building—oily rags, cans of kerosene. It could have been spontaneous combustion. I say, forget it until later."

Miguel gave a dubious grunt. "That building sure looks bad," he said, "half of it charred and all." He grinned suddenly, white teeth flashing in his dark face. "I got an idea. Why don't we shoot a few arrows into the building, scatter some old stuff around in front—that old butter churn on the back porch, the old rusty hand plow behind the barn. It'll look real good to the dudes!"

For an instant, everyone stared at him in stunned disbelief. Then Granny started to laugh, the others joining in.

"Great idea," she declared. "It'll sure add atmosphere!" The laughter died away. "As far as that arson business goes...I can't believe anyone would deliberately do such a thing to us. After all, we don't have any enemies." She rose. "So have we exhausted this subject? Because I have a chocolate cake just begging to be eaten."

While Granny and Niki got the cake, Dani rose and left the room. She didn't want dessert and she didn't want to look at Jack. Every time she did her imagination went into overtime.

GUESTS BEGAN ARRIVING by nine o'clock the next day, with the last ones—two young women from Dallas—driving up a good twelve hours later, arriving hungry as bears. While Granny rustled up a late snack, Dani and Jack got them settled in their cabin.

Hayley Browne, the taller and blonder of the two, had been eyeing Jack ever since Dani introduced them. When he turned to leave, she flung her arms around his neck and gave him a big kiss on the cheek.

"Thanks so much for your help," she cooed. "I'm sure this is going to be the experience of a lifetime!"

Walking back to the main house in the moonlight beside him, Dani asked him a question that had been nagging at her.

"I have the most uncanny feeling that you've met many of our guests before," she said, "especially Hayley Browne. I wonder what the connection is."

He kept his gaze straight ahead. Ever since the fire he'd avoided all personal communication between them.

"Yeah," he said just as they reached the lighted back door. "I've met some of them before."

"Under what circumstances, if I might inquire?"

"A few of them have stayed at the XOX, if you've got to know."

"I see." Or at least, she was beginning to. "How do frequenters of the biggest and most luxurious dude ranch in the hill country end up at the little ol' Bar K, I wonder?"

He turned to face her, the overhead light casting sharp shadows on his face. "I sent 'em here," he said, his tone flat and cool. "The XOX was full up so when they asked for recommendations..." He shrugged. "I can't wait to see what kind of a negative interpretation you put on that."

She bit her lip, resisting the urge to tell him her interpretation: that a full house on the first week would be a real challenge to the neophyte Keenes. On the other hand, he could have thought he was doing them a favor.

So all she said was, "I'll withhold judgment."

"Yeah," he said, "I'll just bet."

DANI THOUGHT SHE KNEW what hard work was before she ever hit Texas, but she'd been fooling herself. Now every minute of the day and many minutes into the night were devoted to pleasing their paying guests. Even Toni, nicest of the nice, sometimes found it hard to keep smiling.

But the guests themselves were wonderful—mostly. The real problem, Dani soon discovered, was the lack of experience of those in charge. In many cases, it was the blind leading the blind.

Except when Jack did the leading. She did her best to stay close to him, to see what he did and how he did it so she'd know how to do it herself when he was gone. He was wonderful, she soon discovered. Not only did the dudes love being exposed to a "real cowboy," but they quickly fell under the spell of his laconic charm—those who weren't already under his spell from the previous year.

Watching him lead the long string of riders out of the corral for the daily trail ride, Dani shook her head in disbelief. Hayley Browne bounced along directly behind him on a short, fat gray mare. She might be a terrible rider, but she dressed the part of a real *drugstore* cowgirl with fringed shirts and tight pants and boots that looked as if they were carved from the hide of some large amphibious creature. Large green stones flashed from the band of her hat.

A happy, laughing line of riders spread out behind, most of them totally inept in the horse-riding department, but having a good time nonetheless. Dani wished she could be with them.

Sighing, she turned back inside the house, where Toni and Granny waited for her in the kitchen. This had to be said, but she sure didn't want to be the one to say it.

Toni took one look at her sister and gasped. "This is something bad, right?"

"I'm afraid so." Dani drew a glass of water from the faucet at the sink to buy time. Then she faced Granny and Toni resolutely.

"I've just balanced our bank accounts and I'm afraid we're in even worse financial straits than we thought."

"Oh, no." Toni looked stricken. "What happened?"

"That big bill for the horses, for one thing."

Granny nodded unhappily. "I'm surprised Jack wouldn't let you pay that off over time," she said.

"He probably would have." Dani bit her lower lip. "I didn't want to be in his debt."

Toni gave an incredulous laugh. "Are you kidding? We *are* in his debt, all of us. Without him, we'd never have got this place opened, and we *sure* wouldn't have a full house."

"You know about that?"

"Of course. Mrs. Headly—you know, in the Doc Holliday Cabin with Mr. Headly, the retired accountant? She told me Jack recommended us."

"Still..."

"Dani Keene," Grandma said severely, "did anyone ever tell you that you have a suspicious nature? Jack's been a godsend, and why you insist on mistrusting everything he says and does, I can't imagine."

"I don't—"

"You do." Toni cut her sister off. "That day we came back and found you two in the John Wesley Hardin Cabin, I thought..." She exchanged a meaningful glance with her grandmother. "Never mind what I thought then. What I think now is that you've let your pride put us in this difficult situation."

Stung, Dani stared at her normally placid sister. "My pride! That's not what this is about."

"Well," Granny said, "if it's about Jack, he's got *my* vote of confidence. Not that I don't have confidence in you, too, dear," she added hastily. "About our financial woes...we'll just have to cut a few corners, that's all. And we know how to do that, don't we, girls?"

Toni nodded, looking expectantly at her sister, who finally nodded, too. There was more Dani could tell them, details that would lead them to the same awful conclusion at which she herself had arrived kicking and screaming:

Barring some miracle, the Keene triplets might

have no choice but to sell the ranch. And judgment day was heading toward them like a runaway freight train.

DANI LED SUNDANCE out of the corral just as Jack and Dylan finished saddling the horses for the trail ride to a steak fry at Lookout Point. Granny, Toni and Dobe had gone on ahead to get everything ready.

Jack looked up from saddling Hayley's gray; each dude was assigned his or her own horse for the duration of their stay and the fat old XOX reject was just Hayley's speed. "You comin' along on the ride?" he asked Dani, obviously surprised.

"I thought I might as well, since everybody else is."

For a moment she thought he looked a tad resentful, but then he nodded and said, "Good. Why don't you take the lead, then."

"All right, I will." Her chin rose another notch. If he thought this was a chance to make her look bad...

But why would he want her to look bad? Maybe Grandma was right and Dani really *was* too suspicious.

Everyone mounted with the usual amount of giggling and laughter and horseplay. When they formed up into their assigned order, Dani was amused to see that Hayley hung back instead of taking her usual spot behind the leader. She nudged her mare close to Jack, who was mounted on a brown gelding. "I thought I'd drop back and ride with you," she said in a sultry tone.

Jack grinned. "And I think you'll get back in line where you're supposed to be," he said cheerfully. "Aren't you the one who said you're only comfortable at the head of the line?"

"Yes, but..." She pouted seductively.

"But, nothing." Leaning over, he gave the gray mare a smart slap on the rear to send her on her way. "I'll see you at the end of the trail," he called after Hayley.

She didn't look as if that was quite what she had in mind. Dani turned away to hide her smile. Apparently Hayley's idea of a good time was *not* riding where she couldn't even see the object of her interest.

"Everybody ready?" Dani called, addressing the motley assemblage milling around in the corral.

"Ready!"

"Then here we go!" Satisfied, Dani led the intrepid band out of the corral and onto a trail clearly marked by years of use. The well-defined path led down to Handbasket Creek, easily forded at that point, then through the trees to a fork in the trail. One branch looped through pasture and woodland while the other led up a series of hills to a picnic and cookout site with a magnificent view of the countryside for miles around.

That was the branch Dani chose, rising in her stirrups and looking back to make sure everyone was doing all right. With Jack riding drag, they certainly were.

JACK LIKED MOST DUDES.

He liked their enthusiasm and their eagerness to try new things like riding horses and throwing ropes, things that must be as foreign to most of them as city life would be to him. He liked their willingness to make fools of themselves and come up laughing.

He didn't like dudes set on finding the "romance of the West" as personally as Hayley Browne did. He'd successfully held her off last year at the XOX, but that had been easy, comparatively speaking, for his duties at the home ranch were considerably more varied than they were here.

Still, she would only be around for a week, so he wasn't too worried. It was almost worth her unwanted attentions to see how much it annoyed Dani.

The trail made a gentle curve to the right, and for a moment he could see Dani leading the parade before she disappeared into the trees. She rode with a familiar ease he could admire. Actually, there was a lot about her he could admire...and a lot he couldn't.

She didn't trust him, obviously, but he had to admit that was mostly his own fault. If only he hadn't had that damned bill for the horses in his pocket! She'd written him a check for the full amount and insisted he take it, but he'd seen the way her hand trembled over the numbers.

The Keene sisters were in a financial bind, no doubt about it. Would they be able to survive on this shoestring? He would gladly lend them money, but—

"Yoo-hoo! Jack!"

Snapping out of his trance, he smiled automatically at the gray-haired grandmother riding a big bay gelding just in front of him. Joan Headly smiled almost as often as Toni did.

"What can I do for you?" he asked.

"You can tell me what kind of tree that is," she said, pointing.

"In Texas, they're cedars. Most other places they're called Mexican junipers." He shrugged with a grin meant to say, "That's Texas."

"And what is that—"

The horse ahead of hers stopped suddenly, distracting her. Simultaneously, all the horses began milling around. Then, from the head of the line, a gray streak burst away, heading south.

Jack spun his horse around, prepared to give chase. Seeing Dani and Sundance take up the pursuit, he reined in his own horse. There was a multitude of reasons to let her do the honors. First of all, she was riding a helluva lot better horse than he was; second, she was the boss; and third...third, Jack had no burning desire to rescue Hayley Browne when there was someone else around who could do it.

Turning back to the confused trail riders, he hollered, loudly enough to be heard by all, "No problem, folks. Dani's got everything under control. You up front, Mike—why don't you lead the way and I'll hang back and make sure everybody's coming? We're almost where we're going so there's no need to hang around waiting for Calamity Jane to return."

This was greeted with general laughter. He could only hope no one would repeat it to either of the women involved.

THE OLD GRAY MARE didn't have a chance against Sundance, even with a head start. By the time Dani reached the fleeing animal her steps were already faltering. It was a simple thing to lean over, grab the reins and pull the horse up, no damage done.

A premature judgment, because no sooner had the mare stopped than Hayley slid out of the saddle—on the wrong side—and sat down hard on the fresh new grass of the meadow.

It was such a funny sight—to see someone decked out like that in sequins and silver sitting there, glaring up accusingly—that Dani couldn't keep from laughing. The expression on Hayley's face quickly wiped all humor away, however.

Dani swung out of the saddle, trying to be solicitous. "I'm sorry," she exclaimed, moving to assist the other woman to rise. "At least no harm was done."

The blonde shook off Dani's helping hand. "How do *you* know? I could have been killed!"

"Oh, I don't think—"

"You certainly don't or you wouldn't have made me ride that horrible animal."

Dani frowned and reached out to snag the gray's reins. "Bessie's one of our most reliable horses," she said soothingly, hoping it was true. Actually, Bessie was one of the XOX horses and Jack had chosen her. "Something spooked her—a bee, a snake, a—"

"A snake?" Hayley shot to her feet, looking around fearfully.

"Back *there*, not here—and I don't *know* it was a snake," Dani said hastily. "It could have been anything. But she's calm now, so—"

"You expect me to get back on that—that animal? After what she did to me?"

Dani kept the pleasant smile on her face. "I'm afraid that's the only way you'll ever get to the campgrounds," she said as calmly and reasonably as she could. Hayley took a limping step and Dani added, "You couldn't be hurt! You didn't even fall off."

The blonde lifted her chin and glared. "I certainly didn't."

Flattery might be the key. "Actually, you handled that ride really well." Sure, on a pet horse with a rocking-chair gait. "Not too many beginning riders could have stayed on." Unless they were drunk and blindfolded. "I'll bet Jack will be really proud of you."

"Jack?"

"He taught you to ride, didn't he?"

Hayley smiled. "He certainly did." She eyed old Bessie warily. "Will you hold that animal still and give me a boost up?"

"Glad to."

Easy enough, since Bessie wasn't offering to go anywhere. Hayley stepped into Dani's cupped hands and lunged into the saddle, hanging on to the horn with both hands.

"Don't go fast," Hayley ordered. She looked scared to death.

"We'll take it nice and slow," Dani agreed, swinging on board the patient Appaloosa. "We don't have far to go so just relax and enjoy the scenery."

"Ha!" Hayley said crossly. Bessie took a step and she hung on even tighter.

What's wrong with this picture? Dani wondered as she led the way back to the trail. Why was Hayley so annoyed when—

And then she knew, although it had practically taken a ton of bricks to make the point: Hayley Browne had wanted Jack to save her. She'd probably done something herself to spook poor old Bessie.

And Dani was the one left holding the bag.

JACK SAW DANI AND HAYLEY ride into the clearing and went to meet them. Everybody else looked up curiously, some with outright glee and others with sympathy.

The short ride on up the hill had passed uneventfully for the rest of the riders. Toni, Grandma and Dobe provided the welcoming committee, complete with tubs of well-iced soda and water, and a fire already smoldering in readiness for the steaks.

Neither of the women seemed any the worse for wear, Jack decided, but with Hayley you never knew.

He lifted his arms and she slid off the gray mare and into them with a pitiful little groan.

"Oh, Jack, it was awful! Why didn't *you* save me?"

His questioning gaze met Dani's over the trembling woman's shoulder. Raising her brows knowingly, Dani grabbed the mare's reins and rode away as if she had no further interest in Jack and Hayley.

Jack tried to disengage himself from Hayley's death grip. "Take it easy," he said. "You weren't in any danger."

"It felt like danger." She did that pouting thing he really, really hated. "I could have been killed."

"Not by old Bessie. Why don't you get something to drink while we wait for the steaks to finish cooking? That'll make you feel better."

"Jack, this is serious!" She all but stamped her foot. "Why, I could—I could *sue* this place!" Her angry words seemed to hang over the clearing, and more than a few of the other guests gave her curious glances before returning to their own pursuits.

Unfortunately, more than dudes had heard the threat. Dani stopped short at the edge of the clearing, her eyes wide with concern.

Well, hell, Jack thought. *What's she thinking now? That this is my fault because I sold her the damned horse?*

JACK SLID ONTO the fallen tree trunk next to Dani, balancing his plate of food. He didn't want to spill a morsel. Grandma Tilly sure knew how to put on a good spread: barbecued steak, beans, potato salad and homemade rolls.

Dani glanced at him, then scooted over to make room somewhat less than enthusiastically, he thought. She didn't say a word.

Settling into his place, he cast her a guarded glance. "You look kinda serious. Anything wrong?"

She shrugged and put her half-full plate on the ground at her feet.

He struggled to get his knife in one hand and the fork in the other without dumping everything onto his lap. "Looks to me like everything's going just fine. All our dudes seem real happy."

"With one possible exception," she said dryly.

"You talkin' about Hayley?" He glanced around until he spotted her, sitting next to Dylan near the campfire. The young cowboy was strumming a guitar and adjusting strings.

"Of course I'm talking about Hayley."

"She's okay," he said carelessly.

"I certainly hope so." Dani stared out over the hills and valleys spread out below this spot. "If she sues us—"

He groaned. "I was afraid you heard that. Look, Dani, that's all talk. She just wanted a little attention."

"I hope you're right."

"I am. If that's all you're worried about..." He frowned. "Is it?"

She nodded, but he wasn't sure he believed her.

"You mad at me because I'm the one who sold you

the horse?'' he asked, trying to make it sound like teasing when it really wasn't.

She jerked her head toward him. "Funny you'd mention that. The thought occurred to me but I...I discarded it.''

"You did?'' He stared at her in pleased surprise. "Does that mean you're starting to get over all those suspicions you've had about me?''

She sighed. "It means I'm trying. I can't promise any more than that.''

Somehow it was enough, just knowing that she didn't automatically condemn him out of hand.

Maybe there was a chance for something to develop here after all.

The question was...what?

10

RUNNING A DUDE RANCH might be darned hard work, but Dani quickly realized it was work she loved. The first group of guests departed and the second group arrived; the following week the process repeated itself, although a few were booked for longer stays. Those holdovers joined the Keenes in the front yard to wave goodbye to those departing.

The process seemed never-ending, and so did the labor, but Dani knew she wasn't the only one enjoying herself. Toni and Grandma went about their varied and many tasks with unrelenting good cheer. Even Niki, who spent most of her time at the Sorry Bastard, pitched in with enthusiasm when her schedule allowed.

Petey fit in as if he were a member of the family. With his own little room beneath the eaves of the attic, he was always under the watchful eye of Dani or Toni or Grandma. Even the dudes looked out for the little boy, treating him, in Granny's words, "Like something on a stick!"

And always, there was Jack.

Dani hated to think about how much she owed him by now...if he was being straight with her. He was the de facto foreman, and she'd begun turning to him for advice and guidance on every aspect of dude ranch life. When nothing else happened that spooked her—no more fires or runaway horses or other potential disasters, no more offers to buy the place—she began to relax.

But not entirely. Her suspicious nature simply wouldn't allow it. Sometimes she'd let herself dream that maybe someday she and Jack might find a way through their own personal hang-ups, but...

"Dani, I found another one of those dang notes." Grandma swept into the office off the dining room, waving what looked like a paper napkin aloft. Annoyance creased her pleasant face. "I swan, that man must have been determined to annoy us from the grave. I found this in the pantry taped to the bottom of that big flour barrel."

"Now what?" Dani accepted the note, opened it and read, "Elsie's trunk's a keeper: flour, bacon, rat cheese. Coffeepot, teapot, chamber pot. If you're reading this I'm ten feet under and you don't know what the hell is going on."

She sighed. "I'll file this with the others," she said, crumpling the bit of paper and tossing it into the trash basket.

"Okay, it's just that..." Granny's frown deepened.

"Just that what?"

"I don't know—just that I feel there must be a method to Wil's madness. He always was wily, but he wasn't crazy."

"You hadn't seen him in more than twenty-five years," Dani pointed out. "Besides, I've been asking around and..." She didn't want to say "Jack says," so she changed tactics. "Folks around here say he was always eccentric, but that after Miss Elsie died he got downright peculiar."

"I can believe it. Sorry I bothered you." Granny glanced pointedly at the books. "Any more bad news?"

Dani closed the ledger with a bang. "Nope. We're doing just fine. Don't you worry about it for a minute." *Let me do the worrying for all of us,* she added silently.

Mollified, Granny nodded and departed. Dani sat there, thinking thoughts she was loath to confront.

Like maybe the reason Jack was being so good and so helpful was because he could afford to wait. That way when the Bar K went belly-up, his family could step in and buy the place without undue hard feelings.

If that's what he thought, he was sadly mistaken.

Shoving the ledger into a drawer, Dani squared her shoulders. She had work to do and she wasn't going to worry about Jack Burke.

"YOU OKAY, Dani?" Watching her walk to the corral, Jack had realized instantly that something was wrong. Which made him royally angry because he didn't like being so sensitive to her moods. She was nothing special to him.

Well, nothing except a good time, but that had happened so infrequently it hardly counted. Except that he couldn't get it out of his head, and every time he saw her seemed to imprint their fleeting moments of passion even more deeply into his brain.

"I'm fine." She let herself into the corral where the horses loitered, waiting to be saddled for the afternoon trail ride.

He followed her into the enclosure. "You don't act fine."

"Sorry." She stopped, her arm around the neck of the black gelding, and sighed. "I was wondering what it would feel like, just once, not to have to worry about money."

He cocked his head and frowned. "You don't know?"

She shook her head slowly. "Not once, not in my entire life. I am so *sick* of pinching pennies and never knowing—" She broke off with a sheepish smile. "I'm sorry, I didn't mean to dump on you."

"No problem." He wanted to go to her, take her in his arms and tell her not to worry anymore, that he'd take care of everything. But this was one thing he couldn't take care of unless he...

Unless he married her. Jeez! He'd almost reached the ripe old age of thirty without marrying anyone. He sure as hell didn't intend to give up his bachelor status because Dani was tired of the struggle.

He grabbed the first handy horse. "You plannin' to lead the trail ride yourself?"

"Yes, I'll do it." Eyes suddenly bleak, she turned to lead the black to the gate connecting the corral with the larger enclosure next to the tack room.

Her disappointment lashed at him.

NIKI JOINED THEM for dinner that night, a rare treat as appreciated by the guests as by her family and the cowboys. Just having her beautiful self in the room seemed to raise spirits.

Not that *she* noticed. Happy and laughing, she leaped to remove dishes from the tables, refill water glasses and fetch dessert.

When Dani protested, Niki laughed.

"I'm a professional," she said lightly, illuminating the room with her smile. "Let me show off for once!"

As if she ever would, Dani thought glumly, watching her sister charm one and all. Toni was just as bad. Every man in the room was captivated with two out of three of the Keene triplets.

Every man except Jack, who seemed distracted and moody. He caught Dani looking at him and his eyes narrowed fractionally, almost as if she had something to do with his state of mind.

"Before anyone leaves..."

Niki's voice intruded on Dani's tense thoughts. She looked up to find her sister framed in the doorway.

When she had everyone's attention, Niki went on. "I want to remind you all that tomorrow night is Dude Night at the Sorry Bastard. It'll be a chance for guests at all the dude ranches in our area to meet and mingle, plus we'll have special entertainment and great Texas munchies."

"Best barbecue in Texas!" Dylan called from the end of the table, where he'd been entertaining a middle-aged lady dude.

Niki nodded. "That's right."

Miguel, sitting next to a Dallas policeman who would have looked at home with six-guns strapped to his hips, piped up. "And the best-looking barmaids in Texas!"

Everyone cheered, everyone but Jack, who rose quietly and slipped out of the room by way of the kitchen. That left Dani behind, bewildered and unhappy.

DUDE NIGHT AT THE Sorry Bastard was not one of Dani's favorite events. Unfortunately for her, the guests all seemed to enjoy it enormously. There wasn't much she could do but go along and pretend to have a good time, since Granny insisted on staying home with Petey. Dobe also declined to go—"I see enough a' them gol-darned dudes right here on the ranch without followin' 'em into town!"

To Dani's surprise, Jack also opted out.

"I'm gonna head for home," he said, standing beside her as several carloads of dudes pulled out to follow Toni to town. "I'll see you tomorrow, Dani."

"Jack." Before he could turn away, she caught his arm, felt the tingle of awareness all the way to her shoulder and pulled her hand away. "Is...is something bothering you?"

"What could be bothering me?" he snapped.

His tone instantly got her back up. "How would I know?" she flung at him. "You've been cross as an old bear lately and I was just trying to be nice. But it's your business so do whatever makes you happy."

He glowered at her. "If I knew what would make me happy, I wouldn't be standing here arguing with you. Have a good time in town, Dani."

This time he really did turn and stalk over to his pickup truck, blast his way inside and peel out of the yard.

Fine, she thought angrily, turning to sit on the porch and wait for her ride into town: one Matthew Vogel, forty-something bachelor computer geek who had to take care of his e-mail before he could leave the sanctity of the Billy the Kid Cabin for the rowdy confines of the local saloon.

This was shaping up to be one great evening.

MATTHEW DROVE HIS VOLVO with absent attention over the dirt roads between the Bar K and town, talking a mile a minute. "And so I'm sure," he was saying earnestly, "you can see how cyberspace and the Internet are changing the way people live and do business all over the globe. My new software program will revolutionize..."

Smiling, nodding, Dani tried not to think about the way Jack had been acting of late. Any tentative camaraderie between them was long gone. When he was around her, he seemed intent upon getting away at the earliest possible moment. Did he somehow sense that she still had her doubts about his role in the problems of the Bar K?

"...and I'm sure you can see how this will impact on..."

Dipping her head in agreement, she zoned out again. Matthew was a nice guy, but not nearly interesting enough to keep her from thinking about the tall, lean cowboy who'd just about taken over her life as well as her thoughts.

"Turn here!" she said, suddenly realizing where they were. "The saloon's on the right in the next block, but you can park around in back if necessary."

"Sure thing." Matthew maneuvered the vehicle around the corner. "...and once this hits the market our next project..."

Heaven help me, Dani thought. *I am in for one long boring evening.*

"LOOK," AUSTIN SAID, "you're drivin' us both crazy. Either set down and eat or go find yourself somethin' else to do."

Jack, who'd been restlessly circling the dining room table instead of joining his father and grandfather in a meal, stopped short, frowning. He said, "Huh?" because he really hadn't been paying the slightest attention to the old man's harangue.

"I said—" Austin's voice rose "—either marry that little gal or get over her."

That caught Jack's attention, all right. "What the hell are you carrying on about?" he demanded. "Who said anything about marryin' anybody?"

"Don't have to say it. I know the signs." Austin looked at his son for support, which Travis gave with a nod.

"I've been there," he said to Jack, "and I know the symptoms. Pa's right. If the only way to get over it is to marry her, then you might as well bite the bullet and get on with it. Because you ain't been fit to live with ever since you took up with the Bar K, and that's a fact."

"I'm not ready to get married," Jack flared, "and *that's* a fact."

The two older men exchanged exasperated glances, and Austin said, "Show me a man who *is* ready to marry and I'll show you a damn fool. Besides, what difference does it makes if you're ready or not? Marriage ain't a life sentence anymore. If you make a mistake—and you will—you can get out of it. All it takes is a little time and a lot of money."

"A *whole* lot of money," Travis agreed, rolling his eyes.

Jack, who'd heard this sorry tune his entire life, stared at his nearest and presumably dearest. "That's downright disgusting," he said. "When I get married—if I *ever* get married—I'll do it right the first time or I won't do it at all."

"Listen to the boy!" Austin threw back his grizzled head for a hearty laugh. "You think you understand women better than me 'n' your pa do? I don't think so! When you been through the mill as many times as we have, you'll—"

"Grandpa," Jack interrupted, "I don't intend goin' through any mill and I *sure* don't intend to get married just because I've got an itch. In the entire history of the Burke family, I don't think I know of a single happy marriage. That's always scared me off but maybe..." He stared at the two attentive men with a dawning realization and added softly, "Maybe I'll be the first."

Spinning around, he headed for the door and slammed out of the dining room. Austin and Travis exchanged knowing glances, and Austin said, "A wink is good as a nod to a blind mule," and burst into laughter again.

EVERYBODY WAS HAVING such a good time that Dani had to wonder what was wrong with *her*. Seated at a table with Toni and Matthew and a happy assortment of dudes, she smiled automatically and tried to force her wandering mind to stay alert.

Niki sashayed up to replace old platters of chips and salsa with new ones. She looked wonderful in jeans, admittedly tight, and a fitted and flowery Western shirt. "Can I bring anyone anything else?" she sang out.

Dr. Coleman, on Dani's left, waved his hand. "I'll have another beer," he said. "June?"

His wife nodded enthusiastically before returning to an animated conversation with the woman on her left. Dr. Coleman glanced at Dani. "How about you, young lady?"

"No, thanks."

He nodded wisely. "Probably a good idea since you're in charge here." He reached for a triangular chip and dipped it into red sauce thick with minced tomatoes and onions and peppers. "Y'know, June and I have been dude-ranch aficionados for years. We spent our honeymoon on one, as a matter of fact."

"Really?" Dani smiled at him. "That's wonderful. How did you happen to pick the Bar K this year—not that we're not delighted."

"Jack recommended it."

If he noticed her sudden tension, he didn't let on. "Jack Burke?"

Dr. Coleman nodded. "When I called to make our usual reservations at the XOX, he steered me on to this place. Said the XOX was full up, which is kind of funny since I'm late making my plans every year and they've always accommodated me before." He shrugged. "Actually, I'm glad, since we're having the best time ever. I suspect we were in a rut at the XOX and didn't even realize it."

"That can happen sometimes." *Jack!* Jack had sent so many guests to the Bar K that he should get a commission. Which were hardly the actions of a low-down polecat, now was it?

Someone leaned against the back of Dani's chair, and she glanced around to find Clevon Mitchell, co-owner of the Sorry Bastard, smiling at the crowd.

"Is Niki taking good care of you folks?" he asked.

Dr. Coleman nodded enthusiastically. "Real good care." He winked at the skinny bar owner. "You've got a gold mine in that girl, sir."

"Don't I know it. Wish I had ten more just like her. And I got Jack to thank for it." Clevon shook his head wonderingly. "Just think, she was gonna waste all that charm serving coffee over to th' coffee shop." He straightened, still smiling. "Anything you folks want, just holler." He moved away.

Dr. Coleman returned to Dani. "All you girls are wonders," he said. "Toni charms everyone she meets and you—" his smile turned mischievous "—you're just one a heck of a cowgirl, if you ask me."

This was supposed to make her feel good? Her sisters charmed everyone they met and the best that could be said of Dani was that she was a *good cowgirl?*

For the first time in her life, Dani was swept with the realization that she'd rather be beautiful and charming than have all the ambition and brains in the world—which she *didn't* have, but she sure had more of that than beauty and charm.

She managed a smile she hoped wasn't as insincere as it felt and murmured a faint, "Thank you," to the doctor.

Who looked puzzled, as if he'd just realized he'd put his foot somewhere in the vicinity of his mouth. "I meant that as a compliment," he said. "Why, I'd follow you anywhere! We all would."

"Thank you," she said again, looking around for some means of escape. Matthew was deeply engrossed in computer talk with the woman on his right, apparently a guest at one of the other dude ranches. "If you'll excuse me, I see someone I need to talk to."

"By all means." Dr. Coleman looked relieved.

Dani stood up. Now what? Both her sisters had been accepted as part of the community, so what was she, chopped liver? She spotted Dylan and made a beeline in his direction.

He looked at her with surprise on his attractive young face. "You look kinda wild-eyed, Dani."

She felt kinda wild-eyed, but gave him what she hoped was a seductive smile. "Care to dance?"

He recoiled. "No, ma'am, I sure don't."

"Dylan Sawyer, I'd like to know why not! I don't bite."

"You sure about that?" He laughed uneasily and added, "That's not the reason, anyway."

"Then what is?" she demanded, nearing the end of her rope.

His smile slid away. "You want the truth?"

The hair at her nape prickled, but she stood resolute. "Of course I do."

"Okay, you asked for it." He eyed her cautiously. "Jack told us not to."

"Jack told you not to what?"

"Dance with you. Or make any moves on you, for that matter."

Her blood pressure skyrocketed. "You're kidding." She stared at him, and then his use of the word *us* sank in. "What do you mean, he told 'us'? Who else is involved in this plot to make me miserable?"

"Us." Dylan's gesture took in the entire room.

"But...*why*?"

"He said it was because you had too much responsibility to be messin' around with some dumb cowboy." He frowned. "Actually...he got all balled up in the why-nots. Then he said you were too smart to have anything to do with us anyway, but later he told Miguel he didn't trust a one of us as far as he could throw us." He grimaced. "Want to know what I think?"

Totally adrift in this long-winded explanation, she nodded.

"I think he's just plain jealous."

"Jack, jealous of me? I don't think so!" And she was annoyed to have it so much as suggested.

"No, think about it," Dylan urged, obviously eager to present some harebrained theory. "Why else would he appoint himself your keeper? You're of age and nobody could say you're not capable of taking care of yourself." He rolled his eyes for emphasis. "*Good* care. I don't know any guys eager to take you on in a shoutin' match, if you know what I mean." His eyes widened as if at a sudden revelation. "Except Jack, of course. He'll take on anybody or anything—anytime."

Was that admiration in the young cowboy's tone? If so, Dani didn't share it. "I don't care what Jack has to say on the subject," she declared, "and I sure don't care why. He's not even here, so I *insist* you dance with me."

"Aw, com' on, Dani, give me a break."

"Don't be a wimp, Dylan! One dance, that's all." She pointed to the dance floor with a stiff forefinger.

"But Jack's my boss and—"

"Jack's not your boss, I am!"

"Yeah, but...you don't understand." He was starting to sweat, figuratively anyway. "I'm just on loan from the XOX and—" Realizing what he had said, he looked stricken.

"On loan from the... You mean you had a job and Jack forced you to work at the Bar K?"

He licked his lips. "Forced is kinda strong for what happened. What he did was promise that if we didn't like it, we could have our old jobs back."

"*We* again, meaning you and Miguel both?"

"Yes, ma'am." He nodded, watching her anxiously.

"Well, that does it." She clenched her hands into fists. "If Jack Burke thinks he can point me any direction he wants by throwing his weight around—"

"Uh-oh."

"Uh-oh what?"

Before he could answer, she looked around and saw the man in the doorway.

Jack Burke, in the flesh. Had he come to gloat?

JACK SPOTTED HER the instant he walked into the Sorry Bastard. She was talking to Dylan, who looked mighty uncomfortable with whatever was going on.

Then she turned, and Jack saw her face and groaned. He was here on a serious mission and she looked ready to spit nails before he even opened his mouth. To hell with that; nothing ventured, nothing gained. Hitching up his wide leather belt, he stalked across the room to the bar.

"Jack Burke!" She gritted her teeth before going on. "I've got a bone to pick with you."

"Okay. I've got a few things to say to you, too. Let's dance." He held out his arms just as if he expected her to fling herself into them.

Which she didn't. "I don't want to dance, I want answers."

Dylan leaned forward. "Two minutes ago you wanted to dance," he pointed out. "Here's your chance." And he turned around resolutely on his bar stool to face the other way.

"Ohh," Dani fumed. "Jack, you make me *so* mad."

"Yeah, I guessed. Let's dance."

"I said I don't want to dance."

"Well, I do!"

They stood there nose to nose, glaring at each

other. Finally she pulled back slightly, said, "What the hell, I guess we can talk on the dance floor as well as anyplace else," and led the way.

Turning stiffly, she stood poker straight while he took her into his arms. Together they moved rigidly into the dance.

After several uncomfortable moments, he said, "You go first."

She started. "Go first where?"

"Talk first."

"Oh." She seemed to have calmed down at least a little. "Okay, I want to know who you think you are, telling Dylan and the guys not to dance with me."

"He told you that, huh?"

"He sure did and I don't like it. Jack, I can't figure you out."

In her agitation, she lost a little of the stiffness and he subtly drew her closer, a move she didn't seem to notice.

He tried a tentative smile. "What's to figure out? I'm a simple man of the West."

"You're a simple man of the West, my eye!" That seemed to jerk her up again. "One minute I think you're on my side and the next I think you're trying to put me and my sisters out of business. What's with you, anyway?"

They danced for another minute in silence while he thought about it. Finally he said, "I've wondered that myself. In the beginning...I really did feel beholden to your pa."

"You paid that debt off forty times over," she scoffed. "There's more to it than that."

"You're not the only one who's said that," he admitted, remembering certain annoying comments from his pa and grandpa.

"Then explain yourself," she commanded. "There is absolutely no reason in the world for you to be messing around in my life this way. Are you trying to make me so miserable that I'll give up and go away? Because even if I did, I'd never let the ranch fall into *your* hands."

"You just don't trust me," he said sadly.

"What's to trust? Every good thing you've done can be taken two ways at least. At the same time, you're involved in every bad thing that's happened." She looked at him with eyes suddenly vulnerable and lips that trembled. "I want to believe you're a good guy, but I guess..."

"Guess what?" He finally succeeded in bringing her fully into his embrace, her body soft and yielding against his at last. His breath caught in his throat. She felt so good.

"I guess I need something...something definitive to put you squarely on one side or the other," she said at last.

The music stopped, but he didn't release her, nor did she indicate any interest in escaping his embrace. "Okay," he agreed. "I'll give you something definitive."

She looked at him with clear hope. "Please do."

He'd come here to do this, but was still uncertain...uncertain that he was doing the right thing. But he *was* going bonkers and this was the only way he knew to stop the slow decline into raving lunacy.

He took a deep breath and said words he'd never uttered before, in a voice that threatened to crack. "Danielle Keene, will you marry me?"

Her eyes flew wide. "Will I *what?*"

"Marry me," he repeated. "Is that definitive enough for you?"

ALL A STUPIFIED DANI could think to say was, "*Why?*"

Jack let out his breath with a disgusted grunt. "Because I love you," he nearly bellowed. "If you were half as smart as the rest of the world thinks you are, you'd have figured that out."

"You...love me?" A melting warmth began to steal through her veins, carrying joy to every part of her stunned being.

"I said so, didn't I?" He glowered at her. "So what part of 'will you marry me' don't you understand?"

"I don't understand any of it," she wailed. "This is so sudden!"

"Sudden, hell." He clutched her tighter. "I've been building up to this since the first day when I saw you at the Y'all Come Café, so you might as well quit stalling." He tilted her chin so he could look into her eyes, his own serious but somehow vulnerable in a new way. "Honey, this is real simple," he said in a voice that beseeched her. "Do you love me or not?"

"I..."

Did she love him? Was that what this wild pounding in her blood meant? Was love the reason she'd rather fight with him than be without him? Was love the reason every molecule of her body shrieked at her to say those elusive words—

"Yes! Yes, I love you, Jack, and I'll marry—"

The rest was lost in his kiss.

THEY HADN'T EVEN GOTTEN through the congratulations and the sisterly hugs before her doubts set in. *Engaged to be married* were just words, words perhaps chosen to throw her off her guard. Did he still have some hidden agenda? They were a long way from married and maybe he was just using an engagement as a carrot on a stick designed to get her to sign something, sell something, do something....

Like make love with him again, for example. If that was what he thought, he'd picked the wrong girl. Because this one wasn't about to fall into his arms until she could be sure.

JACK WATCHED HER accepting congratulations and sly teasing, and slowly it dawned on him that she looked downright uneasy. What the hell? If she really loved him, what was the problem?

But if she didn't love him, why would she accept his proposal? he argued with himself. She'd have no other reason in the world, except...

Her financial situation was desperate and that was harder on her than on her sisters, since she was so much more ambitious. Rather than be forced to sell the dude ranch to the XOX, maybe she'd agreed to marry the heir so she could have her cake and eat it, too.

Damn, that was a cold-blooded thought and he was ashamed of himself for even considering it...but still he couldn't quite push that possibility aside.

At least not until they were celebrating their engagement the good old-fashioned way: in each other's arms on the banks of Handbasket Creek in the moonlight.

SHE HADN'T INTENDED to let this happen again, as a kind of test for both of them. Yet the minute she felt his hand on her thigh on the way home in the pickup, she ignited like a Roman candle.

Whatever troubles they might have, this was not among them. He nearly drove the truck into a tree getting off the road so he could grab her in his arms and start undressing her.

She really didn't intend to help, but found herself tugging at his clothes just the same. Half-naked and all but crazy with wanting him, still she found the breath to complain, "Jack..." It ended in a moan, so she tried again, her head falling back to rest against the seat while he liked and tugged at her breasts. "I can't—not in a pickup!"

He stopped kissing and nibbling at her breasts with obvious reluctance. "I've got a blanket behind the seat. We can spread it on the grass."

So that's how they ended up making love beneath the stars. Drunk with passion, she drifted through the velvety night sky while she gave herself up to his hands and mouth. He touched her everywhere, fondled and caressed every part of her while denying her equal rights to his body.

"This one's for you," he murmured against her belly button, his tongue flicking out to examine the indentation on his way south. "You said you love me and I know I love you. Now I want to make sure neither one of us ever forget it."

When he reached between her thighs, they parted without a struggle. Whatever he did, she was ready. He barely touched her with his fingertips and she was on the verge of an orgasm. When his tongue replaced his hands she exploded.

Spent and trembling, she felt his hardness against her thigh and responded in spite of herself. When he joined their bodies together she caught her breath at the power of it.

Almost at once, she felt another climax gathering deep inside. Clinging to his shoulders and meeting him thrust for thrust, she tried to hold back, anything to prolong the rapture. He responded by moving deeper and faster, and the spark grew into a flame that soon engulfed them both.

Jack shuddered and stiffened above her, then collapsed on top of her with a satisfied groan that mingled with her own bliss.

To think of a lifetime of this kind of fulfillment was almost more than she could handle. Wrapping her arms around him, she whispered words she meant with all her heart: "I'm so tired of fighting. You can have the ranch and everything I own because I love you, Jack, I really really love you—even if you make me crazy at least half of the time."

THEY DROVE ON to the ranch in a kind of sensual fog he was sure engulfed them equally. Damn, but she was a handful. Just thinking about how receptive her body had been made him hard all over again.

He just wished she hadn't tied up her "I love you" with the ranch. He didn't want everything she owned, as she'd put it; he just wanted her, in his heart and his bed for the rest of his natural life. Ah well, he consoled himself, she hadn't meant anything by it. He was imagining things.

He stopped the truck in front of the house and went around to open the door for her. In moonlight nearly as bright as day, he lifted her out of the cab and held her cradled against his chest for a long, slow kiss that curled his toes. She was totally responsive, holding nothing back now. For a nickel, he'd put her back in the truck and drive a hundred miles an hour back to the spot where—

She stiffened and tried to struggle free. He held her, frowning, unable to comprehend what had suddenly set her off. He tried to kiss her again but she turned her head away.

"Don't! Look, Jack!" She pointed.

Groggy with desire, he turned and saw flames

shooting up from the far side of the outbuilding that had nearly burned down once before.

"Son of a—!" Dropping her onto her feet, he dashed forward. What in the hell was going on? "Ring the dinner bell," he called back to her. "We've got to get everybody out here fast!"

He heard her grunt of surprise and then she screamed, "Petey! Jack, it's Petey! What in the world is he doing out here?"

"The dinner bell, Dani! Do it now!"

Jack reached the hose on the end of the bunkhouse, the one he'd used to fight the fire the last time. Twisting the spigot, he soon had a stream of water aimed at the blazing wall.

By the time Dobe, Miguel and Dylan stumbled out of the bunkhouse, Jack nearly had the blaze under control. Passing the hose to Dylan, Jack looked around for Dani—and Petey, which seemed incredible. What the hell was the boy doing out here in the middle of the night, anyway?

He found Petey surrounded by the Keene women and their grandmother. Dani knelt before the sobbing child and spoke reassuringly. "Petey, it's all right. Just tell us what happened."

The boy looked up, saw his uncle and burst into fresh wails. "I didn't do it, Uncle Jack! I didn't light any matches and throw them in that little house!"

Jack's stomach clenched. Petey? Petey was the firebug around here?

Ho-ly sh—!

THE GUESTS POURED from their cabins to witness, and in some cases to help fight, the fire. By the time the last embers flickered out, Dani felt as if she'd been through a wringer.

Standing in the unrelenting glare of floodlights and holding the now silent and subdued Petey by the hand, she fought a terrible sense of numbness. The boy had sort of admitted to torching the building the other time, too—playing, he'd called it. Like many children his age, he was fascinated by matches. Although that revelation horrified Dani, it frightened her even more to realize the boy had slipped out of the house after tucked in for the night by Granny.

That poor old lady was riddled with guilt. "I can't understand how this happened," she repeated over and over as she paced across the yard. "How could I let a four-year-old outsmart me this way?"

"Now, now, Granny." Toni, still clad in a long, white cotton nightgown, patted the woman's shoulder. "It's not your fault. We knew Petey was a handful when he came here. It's as much my fault as yours."

"No," Dani disagreed, "it's *my* fault. I'm the one who brought him here and I should have watched him more closely. I just thank God he wasn't hurt." Kneeling, she pulled the boy against her chest in an enormous hug. "None of the rest of it matters."

Granny choked back a sob. "I guess we'll have to work all that out tomorrow. It looks as if the men have got the fire under control so..." She turned to the hovering guests. "I think I'll make a big pot of coffee—decaf, of course. If any of you would care to join me—?"

That invitation was met with enthusiasm, and the onlookers hiked off toward the kitchen, leaving the triplets and Petey behind to watch the mop-up operation. Jack conferred briefly with the men, who headed back to the bunkhouse while he approached the little group.

"I think it'll be all right now," he said. "Dani, I can't tell you how sorry I am for what Petey did. Just figure out your loss and I'll take care of it."

Holding the little boy's hand again, Dani reached for Jack's. "Don't worry about it. I don't think there was any great loss."

In deep shadows cast by the harsh lighting, his face looked grim. "Don't be too sure," he said slowly. He extended his hand, with something—a piece of jewelry, it looked like—dangling from his fingers.

Puzzled, Dani took the object and held it up before her. Light sparkled from a large dark stone set in the middle of elaborate gold filigree. "What is this?" she murmured in a puzzled tone.

"Unless I miss my guess, it's Miss Elsie's famous emerald necklace," he said.

Dani's stomach twisted. "Where did you find this?"

"In an old, smoldering wicker trunk we pulled out of the fire. And Dani..." He seemed to have trouble going on. "There's more, lots more. I think we've solved the mystery of what Wil Keene did with his assets."

"You mean...?" She could hardly speak, she was so stunned, and her sisters looked equally dumbfounded.

He nodded. Digging into his pocket, he extracted a crumpled piece of paper, which he offered to her. When she released a yawning Petey to take it, Jack took the boy's hand and moved a few steps away.

Turning to catch the light, Dani read, "You girls finally hit the jackpot. Can't trust any damn banks to do the right thing so I'm not taking any chances. Just don't say your old daddy never done you any favors..."

Dani let the words trail off, her gaze seeking Jack's. "How much is out there?" she asked. "Could you tell?"

"Not really. The trunk was stuffed with pots—honey pots, teapots, coffeepots—and every pot was stuffed with money and jewelry. I'd say..." His jaw tightened. "I'd say your money worries are over."

Niki took a stumbling step forward. "Oh, my *God!* I can't believe this!"

"Believe it," Jack said flatly.

"We can get out of debt?" Niki's eyes were wide and wondering.

He nodded. "And then some."

Dani turned to her sisters. "This is a...a miracle," she whispered. "I'd have done *anything* to hang on to this place for the four of us, but I was running out of options."

"Oh, Dani!"

"Oh, Toni!"

"Oh, Niki!"

The sisters fell into each other's arms, laughing and crying at the same time. Dani was so involved that Jack didn't think she even saw him leave with Petey.

IN FRONT OF THE BUNKHOUSE, Petey rebelled. "Uncle Jack, I'm hungry."

Jack looked down at his nephew by the light of one dusty bulb. Petey's lower lip trembled and tears made tracks down his grimy cheeks.

Impulsively Jack picked the boy up and gave him a powerful hug. "Peter Burke, if you ever play with matches again I'll—I'll—I don't know what I'll do, but it'll be awful."

Petey clung to his uncle's neck. "I'm s-s-sorry!"

"You know better." Jack hugged tighter. "How many times have we told you not to play with matches?"

"A million?" Petey burrowed his face against Jack's neck. "I'm s-s-sorry!"

All the anger flowed out of Jack and he loosened his fierce hold on the boy and set him on the ground. "I'm sorry, too," he said. "I'm...sorry about a lot of things."

Into the silence, Petey spoke haltingly. "I want to

go home now, Uncle Jack. Can I go home and get something to eat?"

Jack wanted to go home, too. There didn't seem to be anything left for him here...certainly not love. Dani no longer needed him, so why hang around waiting for her to find a way to tell him?

To Petey he said, "I've got a better idea. Let's go home, pack our bags and go to Disney World. What'd ya say, partner? You've been after me to do that ever since you learned to talk."

"Disney World! Oh, boy! Let's us go!"

And so they did.

WHEN DANI REALIZED Jack wasn't there, she started after him, but stopped short when she saw him dimly illuminated by the light over the bunkhouse door. He was talking to Petey and she probably shouldn't interrupt. But she did hope he wasn't too hard on the boy.

Without Petey, they might never have found the loot stashed by their father. They probably owed the boy a debt of gratitude—although his firebug tendencies needed to be nipped in the bud.

Niki must have noticed her sister's distraction for she slid an arm around her waist. "You can talk to Jack tomorrow," she said gently. "Let him spend a little time with his nephew tonight."

"You're right," Dani conceded, but still she felt a tremor of concern. Jack had seemed upset even after the discovery of the jewels.

Oh, heavens, was he sorry about their good fortune? He must have realized by now that his family would never get control of the Bar K. Did his absence mean he had no further use for her?

Don't be ridiculous, she scolded herself as she helped her sisters haul the charred wicker trunk into the house. *Jack loves me. He said so. Tomorrow I'll realize how silly I'm being.*

But that wasn't what happened, for when tomorrow came she discovered that, in the dark of the night, Jack had taken Petey and left.

THE KEENE WOMEN CAME together the next day to discuss their good fortune. Niki and Toni bubbled with excitement as they examined the contents of Miss Elsie's old trunk: many pieces of old-fashioned but expensive-looking jewelry and more money than they could count with their trembling hands and fragmented attention.

Granny gathered the bills together into a suitcase. "You girls have got to get this in the bank right away," she counseled. "What could that Wil Keene have been thinking of, to leave it out there?"

Niki and Toni looked puzzled, but Dani thought she'd finally figured that out.

"I don't think he was in his right mind," she said slowly. "He had health problems that just got worse the last few years. From what Jack said..." She bit her lower lip. "He was always eccentric, but he got downright strange there toward the end—erratic and unpredictable.

"Perhaps he really wasn't mentally competent," Niki mused. "Poor man."

Dani wasn't ready to go quite that far so she shrugged.

"Speaking of Jack," Toni interjected, "where the heck is he? I haven't seen him all morning. I think we owe him a great big hug for finding this—and of course, Dani owes him more than that!"

They looked at her expectantly and Dani swallowed hard. There was no point in putting it off. "Jack's gone. He took Petey and left."

"To do what?" Toni wondered.

Niki added, "I'm sure there's a logical explanation."

"Of course there is," Dani agreed. "He didn't want me, he wanted the ranch. Now he can't have it, even by marrying me, so he j-just...left." She could barely force out the words and felt even worse when the three of them stared at her as if she'd lost her mind.

Finally Granny said, "You can't possibly believe that."

"I do!"

"Then," Toni said, "you're crazy. Jack loves you. He asked you to marry him, for heaven's sake."

"If he loves me, where is he?"

"Why don't you call the XOX and find out?" Niki suggested. "Then you can apologize to us for scaring us this way."

Dani's chin lifted stubbornly. "Fine. I'll do just that." Marching to the telephone, she dialed the XOX and waited, her entire body trembling.

Jack's grandpa came on the line. "Hello, this is the XOX. Austin Burke speakin'."

"Hello, Mr. Burke. Th-this is Dani Keene at the Bar K. May I speak to Jack, please?"

At the resulting silence, she thought she'd scream.

At last he said, "I hate t' tell you this, but he's gone."

"Gone!" She cast a frantic glance at her family. "Gone where?"

"He took the boy and set off for that Disney World place—Florida, is it? Said he'd be back a week from Friday."

"Did he..." She drew in a deep breath that didn't steady her. "Did he leave a message for me?"

"I'm real sorry to say he didn't." Austin did, indeed, sound sorry.

"All right. Thank you." Dani hung up the telephone and faced her sisters. She wasn't going to fall apart over this. If he didn't love her, then she didn't love him, either. She had no more money problems and she should be happy.

Dammit, she *was* happy!

"I guess that's that," she said, her tone steady even while her heart trembled with grief. "From here on out, it's just the Keene triplets—the three musketeers, all the way."

And for a while, she almost convinced herself it was true.

BY A WEEK FROM FRIDAY, she knew better. After days and nights uncharacteristically filled with lonely tears and meaningless resolutions, Dani Keene had finally come to a conclusion that rocked her well-ordered world: money without love was meaningless.

Big deal, she scolded herself. *Now that you know, what are you going to do about it? Are you going to roll over and play dead or take action?*

But what action would convince him that he was all she really wanted?

Two hours later, she was nailing up flyers all over Hard Knox that read: "Wanted: ONE SPECIAL WRANGLER. Many benefits including room, board, and lots of love from Dani Keene of the Bar K. Must sign on for a lifetime. Only wranglers named Jack Burke need apply."

Then she went home to wait.

And pray.

JACK HAD EXPECTED to return from Florida with a calm mind and a sense of relief that he'd dodged the bullet aimed squarely at his heart by Dani Keene. By the time he'd been home for all of ten minutes, before Petey even got through displaying the mouse-ear hats and bright T-shirts, Jack realized how mistaken he'd been.

"Did she call?" he asked his grandpa.

"Did who call?" The old man observed him with shifty eyes.

"You know who!"

"Oh, her. Yeah, she called right after you left for the airport."

Jack waited. Austin went back to admiring the hat Petey had picked out for his great-grandpa, one with big duck lips on the front.

When he could stand it no longer, Jack yelled, "Well? Aren't you going to tell me what she said?"

"You wanna know that, too? She asked to speak to you, I said you'd gone to Disney World, she said 'thank you' and hung up."

"Just...thank you?"

"What did you expect, boy?" Austin snapped. "You took off on her without a word. Surely you don't expect a girl with that much spunk—"

"Spunk! What do you know about her spunk?"

"Hey, I didn't just fall off a turnip truck." The old man drew himself up proudly. "Way I see it, you got a whole lot of crow to eat if you want that little gal back."

Did he want her back? Jack stared at his grandfather, and all the feelings he'd been fighting so ruthlessly for the last week hit him with such force that he could hardly breathe.

DANI WAS JUST COMING out of the barn when Jack's pickup roared into the yard. He met her halfway between barn and house, both of them stopping a couple of feet short of each other. He looked...grim, she decided.

And brown. She swallowed hard. "You got a nice tan in Florida," she said tentatively.

He shrugged her comment aside. "It's hard not to. Look, Dani, I think we have to get a few things—"

"Don't complicate matters," she interrupted, afraid to let him go on. "You came for the wrangler job, right?" She held her breath; he'd seen her flyer and wanted to make up with her—please!

"You know I didn't come for any damned job, this time or the last time, either!" He looked ready to explode. "You're already trying to replace me? If that ain't a helluva note. Well, I got news for you. This time you're not gonna take advantage of my good nature. It's all or nothin'." He spun on his heels as if ready to walk away from her.

Then she'd take "all"—hadn't the flyer made that clear? Grabbing his arm, she hurried to block his retreat. Fumbling in her pocket, she dragged out a folded copy of her flyer. "What part of 'must sign on for a lifetime' don't you understand? What else can I do, walk barefoot over hot coals?"

He looked as if she'd slapped him in the face. "I swear to God, Dani, I don't know what the hell you're talking about half the time."

Was he being dense on purpose? Hot tears gathered behind her eyelids and she blinked them back furiously. "I don't want just any wrangler, Jack, I want *you*." With hands that shook, she unfolded the flyer and thrust it beneath his nose. "I humiliated myself to let you and the whole town know how much."

He read the words on the paper, then looked at her in confusion. "What is this? You posted this all over town? What are you, nuts?"

"Jack Burke, you take that back!" She rose on her tiptoes, taking refuge in anger. "I'm *not* nuts, I'm in love—with you, you jerk!"

"You love me—really?" He didn't seem able to believe it.

"Yes, dammit. We love each other," she blustered on. "Furthermore, you asked me to marry you and I said yes. I'm holding you to that, understand?"

His eyes widened and he drew a ragged breath through parted lips. "You love me."

"I love you." All the anger and bluster were gone. "I need you so much. Oh, Jack, when you left without a word—"

He took her in his arms then—at long last. "After you found all the loot, I didn't think you needed me anymore," he confessed. "I thought you only accepted my proposal because you needed money so bad."

"What?" She jerked back to glare at him, but then the glare softened. "I confess—I thought you only proposed so you could get your hands on the ranch."

"What?" His glare outdid hers by miles. "I don't give a hoot in hell what happens to this ranch as long as you're happy."

"I'm happy—now." She nestled against his chest, determined never to let him get away from her again.

"In that case, can I ask a favor?"

"Anything."

"Honey, you don't know from nothin' about gettin' good help around here. Promise me that from now on when wranglers are wanted on the Bar K, you'll let *me* handle it."

"Gladly!" Giving in gracefully wasn't nearly as difficult as she'd expected. In fact, she might start to kinda like it...as long as he had his arms around her.

_____ Epilogue _____

DANI AND JACK TOLD Niki, Toni and Grandma their good news just before everyone went in to dinner that night. After much delighted squealing and hugging and even a few tears, the triplets led the way into the dining room, arm in arm. When Dani would have included Jack, he waved off her efforts with a smile and ambled along behind.

"Attention, everyone!" Niki cleared her throat with pompous importance, which was spoiled by her sparkling smile. "My sister Dani has an announcement to make."

Toni pushed Dani forward. "Come on, tell everybody what you just told us."

"Okay," Dani agreed, "but Jack's got to help me."

Dylan banged a fist down on the table. "You two gettin' back together again? Hot dog!"

With Jack's arm around her waist, Dani could laugh along with everyone else. When they'd all quieted down, she said, "You guessed it. Jack and I are getting married." She slanted him a mischievous smile and said off the top of her head, "I think Christmas would be a good time."

"Forget it." He kissed her cheek. "Thanksgiving. We're getting married at Thanksgiving because I'm so danged *thankful* I finally got you to take me serious."

She made a great point of frowning, although her heart was bursting with love. "Jack, I've always wanted to get married at Christmas."

"Yes, and you also wanted to get married when you were thirty but that's not gonna happen, either." He dragged her closer and smiled at their audience. "It's gonna be Thanksgiving. Trust me."

"Christmas!"

"Thanksgiving...darling!"

Granny spoke up. "I've got a better idea, children."

Toni looked relieved. "I sure hope so."

"I do." Granny nodded for emphasis. "I know the perfect date for these two to marry—Halloween. Because the way they carry on, they're sure to have a life full of tricks and treats!"

Laughter rocked the room, but not a soul disagreed, not even the engaged couple wrapped in each other's arms.

Dani thought that sounded really good. From where she stood, the sooner the better!

If you enjoyed what you just read,
then we've got an offer you can't resist!

Take 2 bestselling love stories FREE!

Plus get a FREE surprise gift!

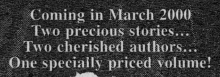

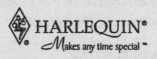

Mother's Day is Around the Corner...
Give the gift that celebrates Life and Love!

Show Mom you care by presenting her with a one-year subscription to:

HARLEQUIN
WORLD'S BEST
Romances

For only $4.96—
That's **75% off the cover price.**

This easy-to-carry, compact magazine delivers 4 exciting romance stories by some of the very best romance authors in the world.

Plus each issue features personal moments with the authors, author biographies, a crossword puzzle and more...

A one-year subscription includes 6 issues full of love, romance and excitement to warm the heart.

To send a gift subscription, write the recipient's name and address on the coupon below, enclose a check for $4.96 and mail it today. In a few weeks, we will send you an acknowledgment letter and a special postcard so you can notify this lucky person that a fabulous gift is on the way!

Every Man Has His Price!

Lost Springs Ranch was famous for turning young mavericks into good men. So word that the ranch was in financial trouble sent a herd of loyal bachelors stampeding back to Wyoming to put themselves on the auction block!

July 1999	*Husband for Hire* Susan Wiggs	January 2000	*The Rancher and the Rich Girl* Heather MacAllister
August	*Courting Callie* Lynn Erickson	February	*Shane's Last Stand* Ruth Jean Dale
September	*Bachelor Father* Vicki Lewis Thompson	March	*A Baby by Chance* Cathy Gillen Thacker
October	*His Bodyguard* Muriel Jensen	April	*The Perfect Solution* Day Leclaire
November	*It Takes a Cowboy* Gina Wilkins	May	*Rent-a-Dad* Judy Christenberry
December	*Hitched by Christmas* Jule McBride	June	*Best Man in Wyoming* Margot Dalton

HARLEQUIN®
Makes any time special ™

Visit us at www.romance.net

PHHOWGEN